HEX
AND
CHOCOLATE
M.J. CAAN

BOOKS

By M.J. Caan

Singing Falls Witches

Hex After Forty

That Good Hex

How Torie Got Her Hex Back

Hex And Chocolate

Moonlight Hexes

Hex And The Single Witch

Hex Education

Hex After Dark

That Hex Factor

Vinci Books

vinci-books.com

Published by Vinci Books Ltd in 2025

1

A CIP catalogue record for this book is available from the British Library.

Paperback ISBN: 9781036705602

The EU GPSR authorised representative is Logos Europe, 9 rue Nicolas Poussion, 17000 La Rochelle, France contact@logoseurope.eu

Chapter One

"Okay. Last chance to back out. Are you sure you want to do this?" Elric's voice was low and gravelly in Torie's ear. She felt her body tense in response.

"Yes. I think I'm ready for it." She had no idea if this was something she would be able to do or not, but her instincts told her it was time.

"You know I don't want to hurt you," Elric said. He moved closer behind her, pushing up against her, each exhale of his breath moved the hair on the back of her neck.

"We've been dancing around this long enough. It's time to see if I can do it. And don't hold back. I'm a lot tougher than I look."

"Relax, don't stiffen up. If you're tense, your body won't move the way it needs to in order to make this work. Don't hold your breath."

Torie nodded and took a deep breath in through her nose, and exhaled slowly, willing the tension in her body to flow out with her breathing.

Then, it happened so fast, she felt panic flood her system as Elric shifted to his hybrid werewolf form and threw his weight onto her.

She let out a sharp grunt as she heard him growl into her ear. His hard, muscular arms closed around her as he grabbed her from behind, pinning her arms to her side.

Torie willed herself to remain calm and trusted her body to respond appropriately. Lifting one foot off the ground, she drove her heel into Elric's instep, while simultaneously snapping her head back, crashing it into his face.

He howled in pain and loosened his grasp on her, just enough for her to raise one fist before slamming it down and back, connecting with his groin. This caused the wolf to break his grip and allowed her to turn and face him. Without thinking, she thrust her hand into his windpipe and then the struck the bridge of his nose with the heel of her hand.

The wolf staggered back, grasping his snout and gasping for air.

Torie retreated, her hands covering her mouth.

"Oh my God...Elric! Are you okay? I swear I didn't mean to lash out that hard." She stepped forward, putting her arm around the wolf as he gasped for breath and shifted back into his human form.

"I'm alright," he said, reassuring her with a smile. "Good thing wolves heal a lot faster than humans." He stood up straight, showing her his nose. The bleeding had stopped almost immediately, and he was no longer gasping for breath. "That was excellent."

Despite her fear that she had hurt him, Torie smiled.

"That kind of felt good," she said. "The adrenaline rush was something I wasn't ready for. But still, are you sure you're okay?" She looked down at his midsection.

"Yeah. That was a stinger, but you need to get used to striking out full strength. So there's no other way to do this."

"Maybe you should wear one of those padded suits... like they do in the women's self-defense class ads I see at the YMCA."

Elric shook his head. "It's not the same. I need to feel what you're dishing out, to make sure you're striking the right way, with the right force to immobilize someone if need be. Besides, believe me when I say; you can't hurt me. Unless you use magic, of course."

Torie smiled, rubbing at a kink in her neck that radiated small twinges of pain into her shoulder. "But I learned a lot about myself when I lost my powers. First, that I can't always depend on them for protection. I need to learn how to handle myself in a crunch. And second, I need to get in better shape. You teaching me self-defense accomplishes both of those things."

Elric moved to stand in front of her. His tall, muscular frame dwarfing her.

"Well, you're doing a great job." He took her hand in his and raised it to the center of his forehead. "Just remember. The most delicate parts of a man, the weakest parts, all run down the center of his body. The eyes, the bridge of the nose, the windpipe, the solar plexus, and of course, the groin." As he named each part, he trailed her hand down the center of his body.

Torie blushed at the last delicate bit. But, in truth, it was more from excitement than embarrassment.

"The hell kind of self-defense is this?" said a voice from behind them.

Torie spun around to see her friend Jasmin standing at the door, hands on her hips.

"Hello, Jasmin. Come on in; it's not what it looks like," Torie said.

"Uh huh. I'm sure. Well at least now I know why you still haven't gotten any furniture. Y'all need a lot of space for all that...defense that's going on."

Elric laughed and moved to a corner of the large living room to retrieve a duffel bag that had been tossed there, along with his shoes.

"No, I don't have furniture yet because I need to experience the space a little more to decide how I want to decorate," said Torie.

Her new home had completed construction just under a month ago. It was a beautiful, traditional two-story with a grand center hall, double staircase that led to the upper level. The house had two separate wings that were angled back slightly from the center portion, offering her a towering, two-story master suite on one side, and spacious guest accommodations along with a study, theater room, library, and a second den in the other wing.

The main hall was dominated by a great room that opened into a massive kitchen with a wall of windows that looked out over Torie's spacious green house and impressive old growth woods beyond that. The upper level balcony contained a loft area with two more bedrooms, each with their own en suite.

It was a grand home, and certainly more space than Torie would ever need.

"I love this house, Torie," Jasmin said. "But are you sure you want to open it up to just any old Tom, Dick or Harry that wanders through?"

"It's not going to be an open house," said Torie. "I just feel incredibly blessed, and I want to give back to this wonderful community that has opened its doors to me, by doing the same. I want everyone to know that if they are ever in a jam, they have a place to stay if need be. Besides, this place is about the same size as yours, and you live alone."

"Hey, don't compare yourself to me. As Madonna said, I am a material girl. I live for luxury. I just figured after everything you went through, and the life you left in New York, you wouldn't go for something like this again."

Torie smiled weakly. "You're right. Honestly, I loved the house my mother lived in, the one I stayed in when first moving here. Part of me wanted to just rebuild it after it was destroyed in that brawl with your daughter…er, I mean, that hunter…but I couldn't. That home belonged to my mother, so I decided I needed to create something that is uniquely mine. I want it to be filled with all the things that are important to me, and what's most important to me is family and friends.

"I want Shawn to feel like he can come here and stay for as long as he wants and not feel cramped. He can bring his friends, maybe at some point a wife and kids. Or a husband; whatever he wants. I want to create something that I can pass on to him and the generation after him."

"And what about a certain werewolf?" asked Jasmin, lowering her voice. "And maybe a houseful of pups?"

Torie mock slapped at her friend's arm. "Jasmin! Stop that. I am way past child-bearing age…so you know that is not happening."

"Oh, I'm just teasing," Jasmin said, laughing. "But seriously, the two of you look very happy. When are you going to make it official?"

Torie blushed slightly. "You never know. Maybe we have plans to go look at furniture this weekend. Together."

Jasmin stared at her friend, a mischievous smile breaking out on her face.

"Girl, you need to tell me everything. But first, you need to go change and meet me at my place so we can head into town to meet Fionna for coffee. She says she has news to share."

Torie checked her watch and nodded. If she hurried, she would just have time to shower and change.

"Elric, I'm going to head into town with Jasmin. Can you lock up?"

"Not a problem," the wolf replied. "I'll see you tonight for dinner. I have a surprise for you."

Torie smiled and blew him a kiss as she walked Jasmin to the door.

"What was that about?" Jasmin wanted to know.

"I don't know. But I can't wait to find out," Torie replied.

Thirty minutes later they were heading into town in Jasmin's blue SUV. The gentle kaleidoscope created by the sunlight breaking in and out of the large trees lining the winding road from the small enclave of houses where Jasmin and Torie lived was mesmerizing.

"You know, I tease you a lot, but Elric is a good man. You lucked out with him," said Jasmin.

"I know. And he is so patient with me. I couldn't ask for more."

"Well, you could ask for a fat ring. Make it official and all."

Torie laughed. "You know, I'm not sure I want to get married again. In the long run, it doesn't mean anything really. If anything, it adds another layer of complication to a good situation; things are going really good with us now."

"Yes, and the enemy of good is better. Still, I'm happy for the both of you. But that doesn't mean I will stop teasing him every chance I get."

"And what about you, Missie? When are you climbing back on that relationship horse? As long as I've known you now, I don't think I've seen you interested in anyone."

"We aren't talking about me. And if we were talking about me, I'd tell you not to go worrying about me. Trust me, my needs are met."

Torie shifted her weight so that she was facing Jasmin.

"So, are you admitting that you're dating someone?"

"Easy there, Nancy Drew. I am a grown woman and what you call 'dating' we grown women call getting ours when we want it."

Torie looked at her appreciatively.

"You know, I love your attitude. You always know what you want and don't bother conforming to what society tells women of our age we should be doing."

Jasmin laughed.

"What society wants is for us to quietly disappear after we turn forty. In some members of society's mind, we are better off unheard and unseen. But you know what? I'm just hitting my stride. I feel better than I did at twenty-five, in mind, spirit and body. Especially body. I know what I like, and I'll tell you a little secret; men like that I tell them what I need. Nobody has time for all that fumbling around and training; I know all the spots they need to hit on my body and in what order."

Torie couldn't help but laugh. "You sound like a teacher."

"Nope. This ride is only for the experienced. I might

take them up a notch, and they just need to hope they can hang. As the sign in my bedroom says, ride at your own risk."

Torie looked shocked. "You do not have that in your bedroom."

Jasmin smiled mischievously. "Okay, maybe not. But I'm thinking about it."

They rounded a curve and saw it at the same time.

A dark sedan had slid off the road, the front end was angled down into a ditch while the rear tires were perched on the dirt edge of the road. The brake lights were glowing red, but the car itself seemed to have stopped running.

Jasmin eased her SUV to a stop behind it, and they both jumped out.

Carefully, Torie made her way down into the ditch to stand beside the passenger door. A man slumped forward, his body resting against the steering wheel.

"Mister! Are you okay?" Torie rapped on the window to get his attention. When he didn't answer, she grasped the door handle and gave it a tug. The door opened and she reached in, gently nudging the man. Still he didn't respond, so she applied a little more pressure and eased him off the steering wheel and back into a sitting position. His head lagged to one side, and it was obvious, even before she laid two fingers on his neck, that the man was dead.

Jasmin gasped, placing a hand over her mouth when she leaned in and saw the man.

"What? Do you know him?" said Torie.

"That's Terry Blatt. He's the town mayor."

Chapter Two

Torie had her phone out and was beginning to dial when Jasmin waved a hand at her.

"Who are you calling?"

"I'm calling 9-1-1. We need an ambulance up here. Then I'm calling Max," Torie said.

"No, call Max first. Give him a head start and then call 9-1-1. I mean, he's definitely dead, so there's nothing an ambulance can do for him."

Torie hesitated but then ended her call and dialed the number for their friend and Sheriff instead. She spoke briefly into the phone and then hung up and placed her 9-1-1 call.

"Okay, everyone has been notified."

Torie watched as Jasmin opened the passenger side door and half entered the car. Then, closing her eyes, she waved her hand inside the car, her lips moving soundlessly. When she was finished, she stood up and looked at Torie.

"Anything?"

Jasmin shook her head. "Nothing. No magical residue,

and I also didn't pick up the latent presence of anyone else in the car with him. He was alone."

"You mean, he just pulled off the side of the road and died? Does that happen to people?"

Jasmin shrugged her shoulders, staring at the dead man before them.

"Maybe he had a heart attack or a stroke?"

Torie assessed the man as best she could. He seemed young and fit to her, and while it was difficult to gauge his height while in the position he was, he appeared to be around five feet ten inches and just under one hundred and seventy pounds.

"Is he even forty?" she asked.

"Unlikely. No one wants the job of mayor in this town, and he pretty much ran unopposed the last two election cycles. He was doing a great job from what I've heard."

Now it was Torie's turn to close her eyes as she reached out with her magic to probe the dead man in front of her. She fought the natural urge to recoil from his lifeless form as her magic snaked in and around the body. She withdrew her power, stepping back from the body.

"I don't sense anything out of the ordinary about the body. He's definitely human, and there are no signs that he died of anything mystical."

"Well, that's good. Cause around here, you never know anymore."

The blare of a siren interrupted them as a black Chevy Tahoe with the letter SFPD Sheriff stenciled on the side in white pulled up. Torie waved as Max stepped out, his gold sheriff's badge glistening in the sunlight.

"Hey, Torie. Jasmin. What have we got here?" he asked, circling the car.

"It's the mayor," said Jasmin. "We were headed into town and came across this."

Max studied the scene, his head swiveling from the car to the road and back again.

"Have you touched anything?" he asked.

Torie and Jasmin exchanged looks.

"Well, I mean…you know, we didn't know he was dead and thought we could help out, so we might have touched the body. But only a little. And once we realized he was dead we haven't messed with him since," said Torie.

Max nodded, noting her nervousness.

"Relax. I just need to make a note of that so we can rule out any DNA you might have transferred."

The two witches watched as he took out his notebook, scribbled something illegible and then resumed his inspection of the car. Putting on gloves, he opened the door and stuck his head inside. Torie could hear him inhaling deeply a few times before he walked back to where she and Jasmin were standing.

"Looks like he's had a few different people in the car with him, but nobody in the last day or so," he said. "Did either of you…er, sense anything odd?"

"If you're asking if he was killed by magic or a supernatural, no," said Jasmin.

Max cocked his head to one side, listening to something they could not hear.

"Ambulance is coming," he said. "You should probably be on your way. I'll let you know if we find anything out of the ordinary."

Torie nodded, just as the wail of the ambulance siren made its way to their less sensitive ears.

"This will be big news in town," said Jasmin. "We'll be around."

"I know you will," Max said as they made their way to Jasmin's SUV and pulled away just as the ambulance came to a screeching halt at the scene.

"What a shame," said Jasmin, shaking her head as they continued down the mountain.

"Did he have family?" asked Torie.

"I don't really know. It wasn't like we were friends or anything. He put in appearances, and was well liked, but at the same time was a loner. Come to think of it, I don't know anything about him that you couldn't find out on his website."

"But he's human, right? And he knew about the sub-community in Singing Falls?"

Jasmin nodded. "He was an ally. He believed in maintaining a peaceful co-existence between the humans and supernaturals. His voice will be missed."

They made the rest of the trip in silence, each sad at the loss of someone they really didn't know.

Fionna was saving them seats at Jim's Bakery, two saucers with cranberry and blueberry scones sat on the small coffee table surrounded by three leather chairs. Torie took a deep breath, inhaling the scent of flour, fresh baked bread, and sweetness of all kinds that always permeated the interior of the bakery.

"Oh, you guys," Fionna said as they approached. "I got your text. Are you okay?" She gave each of them a hug.

"We're alright," said Jasmin. "Better than the mayor, that's for sure."

"So did Max have any idea what happened?"

"None at all," said Torie. "It was really strange." She looked around, setting her purse in her chair. "I"m going to grab a coffee. Jasmin, can I get you one? Another for you, Fionna? Sorry about you having to wait so long for us."

"No, don't even think about it. And I'm fine, thanks."

"I'll have one of whatever you're having," said Jasmin.

A quick trip to the counter and Torie was back, catching the end of Jasmin's remark to Fionna.

"Really, Fionna, I don't think that is what the town is going to be focused on right now."

"Why not? I'm sure I won't be the first one to think about it."

"What are we thinking about?" asked Torie, setting the two cups of espresso down.

"Fionna is worried about the First Eve Festival and if it will still be held," said Jasmin.

"What's that?"

They both stared at her before Fionna's eyes grew as wide as her smile.

"That's right. You've never been here for First Eve! It's a weeklong festival that the town throws every year. It's great; all the shops on main street decorate their storefronts and stay open late to offer samples of their wares. Main Street gets blocked off for sidewalk artists to set up booths as well. There's candy, games, food...so much food! But the best thing of all has to be the chocolate contest."

Torie eyed her suspiciously as the squirrel shifter's eyes rolled back in her head. "I'll have to take your word for it." She laughed happily as she took a sip of her coffee.

"No, seriously, it's the best. You think the sweets here at Jim's are tasty, just wait till you try the ones at the festival. The chocolate competition is open to anyone who wants to enter. You should enter since—" She stopped, glancing at Jasmin.

"Since what?" Torie asked.

Fionna squirmed but didn't answer. Torie looked at Jasmin, arching her eyebrows.

"Well, the winner from the previous year not only gets the best table—front and center—at the contest, but they also get to be the official opener of the festival, along with the mayor."

"Okay," said Torie, "still don't see why I should enter."

"Well, your mother won last year. So you would be continuing the tradition. It's kind of a big honor," said Jasmin.

Torie didn't say anything as she sipped her espresso. She could sense Jasmin giving Fionna a disapproving look and quickly smiled at her friends.

"It's okay," she said. "It's nice knowing that my mother was such a bastion of the community here. I just hope that one day I can live up to her reputation. But I don't think creating chocolate confections will be how I do it." She noticed that Fionna still wasn't looking at her, so she reached over and placed a hand on her friend's knee. "Hey, really. I'm okay. But tell me, why is it called the First Eve celebration? What is the meaning behind it?"

"Well," said Fionna, perking up, "officially, it's the anniversary of the town's founding, when it was established way back in the days of yore."

"Days of yore? Really?" said Jasmin. "You know that was only a little over a hundred years ago, right? I mean, there are shifters in town who probably remember that night. You make it sound like it was a millennia ago."

"Whatever. That's the official reason."

Torie could tell by the way she said it that she was waiting to be asked more.

"And the unofficial reason?"

Fionna's eyes glittered and she leaned in close to the other two women.

"It's the night that a human male and his pregnant wife

were traveling through the area and became lost in a storm. They wandered into the woods and would have died if not for a family of fox shifters who took pity on them. They approached the family in human form and led them to shelter, bringing them food and water. The woman was too weak to continue the trek north, so the shifters suggested they stay with them, just until she was strong enough to continue.

"Then, they insisted she stay until the baby arrived. And by that point, the humans felt like they had found a new home and new friends. There was no need to move on.

"One by one, more human families moved into the little settlement, as well as more shifters. That's how Singing Falls got its start as a tolerance-based community. We accept everyone and believe that everyone deserves a second chance." She glanced at Jasmin, smiling.

Torie wasn't sure what that was about but pretended like she didn't see it.

"Well, that's all very interesting," she said, "but I don't think I'll be entering the contest."

"If there even is one," replied Fionna. "The mayor is the key figure and judge in the celebration. Without him, I wonder if the town will even hold the festival."

Torie didn't say anything as she resumed sipping her drink. Then her eyes widened as she remembered something.

"Fionna, what was it that you had to tell us? You said you had news you wanted to share."

"Yes, what was it that had you all worked up?" asked Jasmin.

Fionna had a sheepish look on her face.

"It seems so silly now. Especially in light of what just happened with the mayor," she said.

"Oh nonsense," said Jasmin. "Go ahead. Tell us."

Fionna pursed her lips then leaned in, eyebrows arched, like she was about to divulge the greatest secret in existence.

"Okay. I'm going to be having a birthday party!"

She delivered the news and sat back quickly into her chair, hands clasped together in excitement.

Torie blinked. "That's it? You're having a birthday party?"

Before she could continue, Jasmin was on her feet, wringing her hands in amazement as her face lit up in delight. She grabbed Fionna and gave her an enthusiastic hug.

"Girl, yes! I am so happy for you!"

Torie was all for birthday celebrations, but something about this seemed a little off from what she was used to.

"Am I missing something?" she asked.

Jasmin beamed, her smile lighting up the coffee shop. "She is celebrating her birthday! Do you know how big this is?"

Fionna rolled her eyes. "Of course she doesn't. How could she know?" They both sat down and stared at Torie before Fionna continued. "Shifters don't have birthdays. That's a human tradition."

Torie was genuinely confused at this point. "What do you mean you don't have a birthday? Everyone has a birthday."

"Technically, yes. Obviously, I know that I was born. But I don't know what day. It isn't something that a shifter celebrates because there is no meaning tied to it for us."

"So, if you don't celebrate your birthday, or know when it is, how do you know how old you are?" asked Torie.

Fionna shrugged. "I have no idea how old I am."

"And why have you chosen to adopt this human tradition now?" asked Jasmin.

"It was Glen's idea. She is really keen on me having a special day dedicated just to me. She has asked me to consider it for years, and now, lately, I've decided why not? Each year I am with her I'm reminded that, while we aren't promised forever, I can't imagine a future without her. So, if making me celebrate the passing of another year successfully makes her happy, then it makes me happy too."

Jasmin clapped her hands wildly. "I am so happy to hear that. Of course, it could also mean that you're taking one more step towards embracing life with humans a little more."

"Well, considering I'm practically married to one, I don't see how it could hurt. But anyway, that was my news. Kind of pales in comparison to what you guys just experienced."

"Well, a dead mayor does not take precedence over a best friend's first birthday!" said Jasmin. "We are throwing you a birthday party. When have you decided your birthday will be?"

"Two Saturdays from tomorrow. It will be the day before the kickoff to the Festival."

"This will be so much fun," said Jasmin. "You leave everything to us. You just show up and be ready for an amazing evening."

Torie smiled as she watched her two friends. The fact that they were experiencing so much joy over a yearly event that she had come to dread, told her she still had some baggage to unpack over her own ideas around age. She might not like marking the passage of time, but she couldn't imagine not having that day to dread.

She caught Jasmin giving her a questioning look out of

the corner of her eye, but before she could say anything, she saw the front door to the bakery swing open as Max entered the building. He scanned the room before setting his dark eyes on the three women and then made his way over to them.

"Hi, Max," said Jasmin. "Please tell us you found out what happened with the mayor."

He shifted his weight from one leg to the other before reaching into his pocket.

"I did find something, just not sure what it means."

He withdrew a folded piece of paper and placed it on the coffee table in front of them.

Written on the paper in red ink was a single name, and underneath that, a phone number.

The name was Torie Bliss; underneath was her cell phone number and address.

"Would you happen to know why the dead mayor of Singing Falls had your name and contact information in his pocket, Torie?"

Chapter Three

Torie looked genuinely dumbfounded. She stared at the piece of crumpled paper, then swept her eyes from Jasmin to Fionna and back to the paper.

"I have no idea. I didn't even know the town had a mayor until Jasmin told me who he was."

"And yet, he has your personal information with him. Could it be that he was on his way to see you? His car was facing north after all, which would suggest that he was headed up the mountain."

"Max," said Jasmin, "why are you trying to make a connection where there is none? She already said she didn't know the guy."

Max leveled his gray eyes at the women. "Because I basically tampered with evidence to get this before anyone at the coroner's office found it on him. I'm risking this badge bringing it to you. I'm not your enemy here, but I need you to keep me in the loop with whatever the three of you may be up to."

Torie rolled her eyes in exasperation. "We aren't up to

anything, Max. We were on our way here to meet Fionna and we happened to drive past a car accident. We stopped to see if there was anything we could do to help, and well, you know the rest."

"So, unless you're trying to say Torie had something to do with the mayor's accident, then you need to be on your way," said Jasmin. She stood, hand on hips, as she met the werewolf's steely gaze. "Honestly, I have half a mind not to invite you to Fionna's birthday party for this."

Max looked over at Fionna, eyebrows arched. "Birthday? Really?"

She smiled and nodded. "It will be my first, so I want to share it with all my friends."

Max seemed a little startled by her words. "And you consider me one of your friends?"

Fionna laughed. "Of course, silly. How many times have you saved our lives? Yes, you are my friend."

"Okay, to be honest it's probably about even in the life saving department," said Jasmin. "But right now, you need to get back to the investigation with the mayor and let us know what you find out." She saw the quizzical look Max gave her and sighed deeply. "Fine. We will also let you know if we find out anything as well."

"How's Elric?" asked Max, turning to Torie.

"He's fine. He's going to help me pick out furniture for the house. Then I'm having a big dinner for everyone to break the place in."

Jasmin and Fionna looked at one another, eyes lighting up at the same time.

"I have a great idea," said Jasmin. "Why don't you host Fionna's birthday party? Your place is big enough for any size gathering, and you can consider it a housewarming party as well."

Torie thought for a moment. "Sounds good, but I don't want to steal anything from Fionna's special day. I don't want it to be about anything other than her."

Fionna waved her hand, shooing Torie's words away. "Oh no worries. I've never had a birthday, so I don't know what to expect. Plus, I'm dying to see what you and Elric are going to do to y'all's place."

The fact that she referred to it as being 'theirs' didn't escape Torie, but she didn't say anything. She just smiled and nodded. Truth be told, thinking of it as theirs did bring a warm, fluttering feeling to her stomach. She eyed Max sheepishly.

"Well, we'll see about all that. But yes, I would love to host," she said. She furrowed her brows. "I'm just not sure that I'll be able to get the furniture picked out and delivered by then."

"Of course you can. I gave you the name of my designer. She can get it done, just give her a call. I mean, it won't be cheap; but it will be worth it," said Jasmin.

Torie stood up, finishing off her coffee. "In that case, I should probably get going." She turned to Max. "Let us know if we can help with the investigation involving the mayor. I really would love to know why he had my contact information."

"You and me both," said Max.

"Torie, if you're going to have guests over, we need to finish our own special project at your house," added Jasmin. Her voice was deliberately cryptic and triggered something in Torie.

"Oh yeah. Let's head back to my place and get that over with."

Fionna said nothing, and Max gave them both a questioning look before offering a shrug.

"Say hi to Elric for me," he said. "And I'll call you later to let you know if I find anything."

With that he was gone, making his way out of the bakery to his black and blue SUV that doubled both as his personal and work vehicle.

"Okay, well, you two go off and do whatever witchy work you have to do," said Fionna. "I've shopping to do for dinner tonight. Glen is sleeping off a double so she will be starving when she wakes. I'll talk to you later."

They all stood with the shifter and made their way out to the sidewalk in front of the building where they exchanged hugs and well wishes. Fionna headed off, digging into her pocket to review a shopping list, while Torie and Jasmin headed back to Jasmin's car.

"So," said Torie, "are we headed for the mayor's house?"

"What? No, we are going back to your new place to finish blessing it. What did you think I was talking about?"

Torie pursed her lips. "I thought maybe you were hinting that we were going to go nose around the mayor's place to see what we could find."

"Girl, why are you so nosey?" Jasmin laughed. "I really did mean we need to finish up at your place."

Torie smiled and nodded as she climbed into the passenger seat, fastening her seatbelt.

"But then, I was thinking it wouldn't hurt to head over to the mayor's house and see if we could dig up anything that might help Max."

Torie broke into a smile and looked at her friend.

Jasmin rolled her eyes, started up the car and backed it out into the street.

"But you're still nosey," she said, not looking over at her friend.

"So, tell me again, what is the purpose of this?" asked Torie.

The two witches were standing in the great room of her new house, just below where the two staircases joined to form the loft area of her home. Torie had consulted Jasmin in the building of the house, and Jasmin had instructed her and her architect to make it the center most point of the home, a spot that was equidistant from all other points in the massive house.

"Look, after everything that has happened since you moved to town, I think you need to make sure you are as protected as possible," said Jasmin. "For whatever reason, you attract trouble unlike anyone I've ever known. The fact that your last home was practically demolished by a fight between werewolves, shifters and a hunter are proof that we need to make sure history doesn't repeat itself. This is a brand-new build, no residual energy from previous owners and it hasn't had time to observe any latent energy that resides in the earth around here.

"It's a blank canvas. Perfect for installing apocalypse level shields and repellants."

"Repellants?"

"Yes. Think of them as industrial strength wards. On steroids. You know why the great pyramids have lasted so long? They are stone that has been reinforced by spell and ritual for hundreds of years. We are going to use those same reinforcements on your house. To keep those unwanted terrors that seem to be attracted to you at bay."

Torie frowned. "Are you saying the great pyramids of Egypt were built by witches? I find that hard to believe."

"Well, you never know. Could have been," Jasmin

replied with a wink. "At any rate, we are going to shore up your house with wards that will penetrate every inch of the place. Nothing nefarious will be able to pass through whether you are here or not."

"Wait, are we going to have to sit on the floor again?" asked Torie. "Cos I don't know if I'm up for that."

Jasmin sighed. "If you didn't spend all morning playing Buffy with Elric, your joints wouldn't be so stiff." She looked around. Waving one hand in the air, she summoned the large pillows from Torie's bed to appear before them.

She dropped to the floor, sitting cross-legged on one, and motioned for Torie to have a seat on the other across from her.

Torie sat, taking mental note of the groan that escaped her lips. When did that start? To her ears she sounded like a stereotypical, nine months pregnant woman from television shows. She made it a point to never make that sound again.

Looking up at Jasmin she felt her cheeks grow red. "What? It's my knees. Too many sports as a teenager."

"Um hm. I guess it's bad when you make the same sounds sitting down that you do during sex." Torie eyed her with a steely gaze but said nothing. "So, we have already blessed the house. Making sure there is no negative energy in the space; cleansing it of any impurities that may have seeped in during the building process. Now, we need to address the very bedrock this house is built upon. Speaking of, you did have them build the foundation and the first floor out of local bedrock, didn't you?"

Torie nodded. "I did. It added a lot of expense, but I trust you when you say it is worth it."

"The rock in this area is steeped in residual magic from the ley lines that run through Singing Falls. That magic will help make the house even more powerful over the years."

She closed her eyes and placed her hands, palm up, on her knees. Torie mimicked her, freeing her own magic to reach out and join with the energy that Jasmin had tapped into.

Slowly, Jasmin began to chant.

"Bright Lady, come guide our hand,
strengthen the land on which we stand.
By sun and moon and force of will,
let none enter this space whose intentions are ill."

Torie joined in, picking up the spell and repeating it in tandem with her friend.

Slowly, as the two chanted their spell, the air between them grew thick with magic. Magic that began to spin and weave itself around the space between them before coalescing into a single, glowing red ball that swirled and sparkled.

The witches used their hands, being careful not to touch the magic, to mimic the rotation of the spell as they guided it down and into the floor between them. The globe sank into the flooring, causing the entire room to glow as it slowly sank into the wood, settling into the ground beneath the house.

Both of them exhaled once the spell was complete.

"Now, all we need to do is repeat that on the first full moon of each month for a couple of months, and this place should be a mystical safe house for you," said Jasmin.

"You mean for us," said Torie. "This house will be a stronghold for all who step foot inside. We have both made some enemies lately...there's strength in numbers with us."

Jasmin smiled, opening her mouth to speak, but she was cut off by the beeping of Torie's cell phone. She looked at the name that popped up before placing it to her ear.

"Hey, Max, what's up? What? Slow down…when? Okay, we are on our way."

"What is it?" asked Jasmin. The change in Torie's body language told her something was very wrong.

"Max is at the mayor's house. Apparently, he received a call that there was a dead body. One that started moving once he arrived on scene."

Chapter Four

The mayor of Singing Falls lived in a well-manicured, secluded Tudor-style home in one of the more established communities of the small town. This particular enclave of homes had been built back in the sixties with a few of the houses showing signs of recent renovation. The subdivision was comprised of stylish ranch and two-bedroom homes that were modest and comfortable. Like many of the houses built at the time, they had something that the newer builds did not; land.

Each home sat on nearly an acre of land that was sculpted and hidden behind rows of shoulder-high hedges and long, winding driveways.

Jasmin parked behind Max's police SUV and then walked to the large, gray wooden door that was flanked by large picture windows. Max was waiting for them on the porch.

"Max, what's going on?" asked Torie. "Where is the ambulance? Where's the body or non-body you found?"

The large sheriff held up a hand to slow her down.

"Easy. I was first on the scene; beat the ambulance here. I sent them away."

Jasmin looked back at the drive. There were no other vehicles onsite. No police backup, no rescue and no medical examiner. She looked questioningly at Max.

"A call came across the wire from Frederica Morris," he said.

"The realtor?" asked Jasmin.

"And town busybody," said Max.

If town gossip was an actual calling, then Frederica would have been canonized at this point. She was harmless for the most part but often made it her business to know everyone else's business in Singing Falls. She was a social butterfly, flitting from garden party to dinner party, repeating anything half worthy that she may have picked up during her day's travels. She also just happened to be one of the best real estate agents in town. The only thing she liked better than a bit of hot gossip was hearing someone mention they were thinking about selling.

"She said she dropped by the mayor's house just to check on things and make sure it was all locked up," continued Max.

"Um hm. You mean she came by to see what shape it was in so she could get a jump on listing it, probably," said Jasmin.

Max smiled, nodding. "Anyway. She says the door was unlocked so she just stuck her head in. That's when she said she thought she heard a noise coming from somewhere upstairs in the house. She went to check it out and she found…well, come with me. I'll show you."

The three of them stepped inside the well-maintained home. Inside, the house looked more like a center hall colonial with a central staircase that greeted them and rose gracefully to a landing on the second floor.

"Where is the woman who found the body?" said Torie as they started to ascend the stairs. "Ms…what was her name again?"

"Frederica," said Max. "She's up here in the second bedroom. She had a fairly powerful reaction to seeing the dead body start to move. She fainted, so I placed her in another room, gave her some water, and asked her to stay in there."

"You keep referring to a dead body. But then you say she moved. Are we talking zombie here?" asked Jasmin. "Why would you call us?"

"Well, I didn't call you for zombie reasons, but yes, your skills are needed."

He led the two witches from the landing and down a hallway that opened into the master suite. The room was nicely appointed with a matching set of furniture arranged against two of the walls. The third wall had a bed placed against it, and on that bed, they could see the tiny, frail figure of a woman.

She lay on her back, dressed in a white, silk nightgown. Her skin was an unhealthy shade of pale, made all the more garish by the roughly applied red lipstick and blue eye liner that had been laid on a little too thickly. There were patches of rose-colored rouge that had been dabbed oddly on her cheeks in uneven amounts as well.

Her hair was completely silver and fanned out over the pillow. Her hands were crossed over her abdomen peacefully as if she were sleeping…or dead.

Jasmin peered closely at the woman. "She looks dead to me," she said.

Max was standing there, arms folded. "Looked that way

to me as well. But..." He leaned over, placed a hand on the woman's shoulder and gently shook her.

The woman gasped slightly, her red lips parting just enough to let out a tiny puff of air. She struggled to lift her arms, and that was when the witches saw it; a small wisp of black smoke appeared around her tiny wrists as she attempted to lift them. The smoke pulled them back together, securing her arms against her belly as she sank back into the bed, motionless.

"The hell just happened?" demanded Jasmin, jumping back.

Torie's eyes grew large as she stared at the woman.

"Was that magic? Is she bound?"

"Now you see why I called the two of you instead of 9-1-1," said Max.

Jasmin went to one side of the bed and Torie the other. Stretching her arm across the woman's body, Torie closed her eyes and reached out with her own power.

"It's weird," she said. "I feel something...but it's so faint, so far away."

"Yes. It's also different from anything I've ever sensed," said Jasmin. "It's almost like some kind of dormant spell; just waiting there. Max, what do your senses tell you?"

The wolf stepped closer. "I could smell residual magic of some kind when I stepped into the room. But it was so faint, I really didn't think anything about it. But I knew she wasn't dead, more like in a very deep sleep. Her heartbeat is very sluggish and weak. I can see why Frederica thought she was dead."

"Dormant," said Torie, "just like the magic we can feel."

"I wonder..." said Jasmin, her words trailing off as she leaned over the woman, placing her hands on top of the frail, wrinkled hands that moments before had been held in place by darkness. "Maybe dormant isn't the right word. I don't feel anything at all now. Maybe, whatever spell is holding her in place, only flares to life when needed."

Torie was nodding. "Like when she becomes agitated and tries to get out of bed."

"That's what I'm thinking. If Frederica touched her the way Max just did, and it roused her, that might be why Max could smell the residual magic when he came to the room. It came to life, did its job of binding her, and then went dormant again."

Torie and Jasmin exchanged looks.

"Max," said Torie, "when we give you the signal, try to rouse her again."

The witches reached forward, holding their hands over the woman's body. They closed their eyes and when they reopened them, they glowed with power.

Torie nodded her head at Max, and the wolf once again gently nudged the woman. The response was almost instantaneous as again her eyes flew open and she gasped for breath.

This time, when her hands fluttered, activating the mystic restraints, Torie and Jasmin were ready.

Moving fast, they grabbed the ethereal smoke that appeared around her wrists, wrestling with the power.

Max could hear them chanting under their breath as they moved in unison, twisting the blackness, trying to draw it off the woman.

Beads of sweat broke out on Torie's forehead as she applied her own magic against that of the bonds. Slowly, together, they were able to pull the dark binding away from the woman and encase it in a globe of white magic that floated above the body between them.

It looked like a writhing mass of angry, smoky snakes entrapped in a glowing ball. The blackness struggled against the entrapment spell, striking out at the walls of its containment.

"That was harder than I thought it would be," said Jasmin.

Torie nodded in agreement. "What is that?"

"I don't know. But it's powerful magic. Not something we want to leave around either."

Together, they held out their arms, hands inches away from the globe that held the writhing darkness, and they chanted.

"Mother of night, steeped in lore,
let this darkness be no more."

The darkness fought, resisting the power of the witches, but in the end, it proved no match for their will. Light consumed it within the confines of the globe, sparking and eating away at it until there was nothing left. Only then did they release their power, dissolving the globe away.

"Have you ever known the mayor to work in magics before?" asked Torie.

"Never. He's never so much as set off a blip on my radar. This came from someone—or something—old and powerful."

Before either of them could speak another word, a small moan escaped the woman lying on the bed and she began to roll her head slowly from side to side on the pillow. A small tear ran down her cheek.

"Thank you," she said, her voice nothing more than a cracked whisper. "I...I...where am I...?" She was confused and quickly becoming distressed.

Torie placed her hand on the old woman's, caressing it gently.

"You're okay. My name is Torie. These are my friends, Jasmin and Max. We aren't going to hurt you. We're friends."

The woman tried to draw away, fear creeping over her features.

"Please, please don't hurt me anymore. I'm sorry for whatever I did…just don't hurt me."

Torie felt her heart break for the woman. What the hell had been going on here?

Jasmin softly stroked her hand as well. "No one is going to hurt you. We are here to help."

The woman turned her head toward Jasmin's voice and struggled to open her eyes.

Jasmin gasped at the grayish globes that tried to focus on her.

"Dear God, she's blind," said Jasmin. "Max, get her some water."

The Sheriff left the room quickly, running into the adjoining bathroom. He returned with a small paper cup filled with water.

Torie slipped her arm around the woman's neck and gently eased her head off the pillow. She took the cup from Max and brought it gently to her lips.

"Careful…slowly," she said as the woman sipped the water. When she was finished, Torie dabbed at the drops that escaped the sides of her mouth and smiled at the woman. "There. That's better, isn't it?"

The old woman nodded and raised a hand in Torie's direction. Torie took her hand and held it. She appeared to be more bones than flesh, and her grip lacked even the strength of a child. Her skin was paper thin, and Torie was careful not to grip her too tightly lest she tear it.

"Do you know where you are?" asked Torie.

"I...I'm in my bedroom, I think. At least that's where I remember being."

Torie and Jasmin exchanged worried looks. Max took out his small, spiral-bound notebook and began scribbling in it.

"Your bedroom?" asked Jasmin. "Do you know how long you've been here?"

The woman frowned. "No. I don't remember. But I'm sure I'm in my bedroom."

Torie looked about, and that was when she noticed how meticulously clean everything was. Everything was arranged and organized obsessively. There was nothing cluttering any of the nightstands in the room, and the one next to the bed only held a single, digital alarm clock. Jasmin opened the top drawer of the stand and found a single book resting there. It was a bible. In braille.

"Ma'am, do you know Terry Blatt?" asked Jasmin. "Mayor Terry Blatt?"

The woman's brow furrowed. "Well of course I do. That's my son. He's the mayor of Singing Falls." She stopped speaking, her gray eyes grew larger, and her small mouth opened to a wide O. She shook her head from side to side, becoming visibly more agitated.

"No, please...no. Terry, don't do this to me again. I'm so sorry for whatever I did, but don't lock me in again. Please." She grabbed fiercely at Torie's hand, pulling desperately at the witch. She was quickly approaching panic, and Torie feared for the woman's health. "Don't let him do it to me again," the woman pleaded.

"Shhhh," said Torie, stroking her hair to try and calm

her. "No one is going to do anything to you. We're going to make sure of that and we're going to get you some help."

The woman seemed to calm down a bit as she rested her head back on the pillow, not letting go of Torie's hand.

"Please don't let him hurt me again..." her voice was once again weak and raspy.

Max took out his phone, sending a quick text message before placing it back in his pocket.

"Who are you contacting?" asked Torie.

"Glen. This woman needs medical clearance before we can get her out of here. Until we can piece together what is going on, I don't think we should wheel her into a hospital. Besides, she seems pretty attached to you." He moved to leave the room, only to be stopped by Jasmin.

"Where are you going?"

"To check on Frederica. I need to make sure she doesn't go running around town spouting off about what she *thinks* she saw."

Torie nodded. "Good idea. But once Glen is finished with her, what are we going to do?"

"Well, that's easy," Max said, walking out of the room. "She can stay with you until we figure this all out."

Torie opened her mouth to protest, but nothing came out. She looked down at the bony figure lying on the bed and then up to Jasmin.

Jasmin shrugged her shoulders and smiled.

"Guess we better move up that furniture order."

Chapter Five

"She's malnourished, but not dehydrated," said Glen. The nurse anesthetist turned first responder, folded her stethoscope and placed it in her red medical kit as she finished her examination of the old woman. "Despite everything, she seems in relatively good shape. Whoever did this to her at least gave her water. I am concerned about the bed sores on her backside, however. She's been lying like this for a while to develop those."

Anger swelled in Torie's chest. "How long has she been like this?"

Glen took a deep breath. "No way to tell for sure. But I'd say a few weeks at least. But the muscle deterioration she is showing would suggest much, much longer."

Max walked back into the room, closing the notebook he had been scribbling in. "Just checked records at City Hall. There is no record of the mayor having a mother listed as living."

"But what about her claims that this is her house?" asked Jasmin.

"Checked that as well. The house is in his name. Bank records show there was never a mortgage; place was bought and paid for in cash."

"This just doesn't make sense," said Torie. "If she isn't his mother, then who is she?"

"Why don't we just ask her?" said Glen. "She seems perfectly lucid and is responding well to the nutrients I've got running."

Torie agreed and moved to sit next to the lady. She placed her hand gently on the woman's forearm, just below the insertion point of the intravenous catheter Glen had placed. It was fed by a bag of fluids that hung from the tall bedpost at the head of the bed.

"Hi there, do you remember me?"

The woman's sightless eyes turned in Torie's direction. "Yes. Torie, right?"

Torie smiled. "Yes, that's right. You seem to be feeling much better."

"My back aches. I feel sore all over."

"We are going to help you with all of that. But first, we need some information if you could help us. Can you tell us your name? Do you know it?"

The woman's eyes grew large with surprise. "My name? Of course I know it. I'm old, not senile. My name is Effie. Effie Kandan. And this is my house."

Torie looked over at Max who had written her name down and left the room. She heard him descend the stairs as he headed for the computer in his SUV.

"It's nice to meet you, Effie," Torie said. "Effie, do you know how long you've been lying in this bed?"

Her gray eyebrows furrowed together, and her mouth moved silently as she seemed to be counting to herself.

"Well, I'm seventy-six years old and if I remember, my son put me here shortly after I came for a visit."

"And when was that?" asked Torie.

"Eight years ago, I believe. I lived with my sister until then."

Torie sucked in air and looked at Jasmin and Glen. Glen frowned, shaking her head as she whispered to Jasmin.

"Effie, are you saying your son has kept you in your bed for eight years?" asked Jasmin.

"No, not the entire time. He locked me in my room first. He only confined me to my bed a couple of months ago, I think. But it's hard to remember that. I feel like I've been stuck in a dream for some time and am only just waking up."

Torie swallowed hard, her empathy for the woman mixing with her anger for the son.

"Where is Terry?" asked Effie, she seemed startled, almost as if she were only just remembering the man who had done this to her. "He hasn't been around lately. He always brings me my tea and we watch my shows together."

Her voice was fading, and Torie could tell that she was slipping back into memories of a time before whatever had led her to be in this position.

She gave a quick glance to Jasmin before leaning in to comfort Effie. "We are going to try and find out what happened, and we will look for your son as well."

She had no idea why she lied to the woman, other than to protect her from more pain. She knew that at some point they would have to tell her that her son was dead, but she didn't think Effie was in a place to hear that just yet.

Effie closed her eyes and seemed to relax, drifting off to sleep. Torie let go of her arm and moved to join her friends just as Max returned to the bedroom.

"No luck on the name Effie Kandan. At least not locally. I fed her name to a friend of mine down in Trinity that has access to a larger, nationwide database. We'll see what that turns up. You get anything else out of her?"

"She said her son has kept her locked away in here for eight years," said Jasmin, looking sadly at the frail older woman.

"I don't see how that is possible," said Glen. "She's clearly not as in command of her faculties as I thought. She's confused; not realizing how much time has passed."

"Could she have been lying in this bed for months?" asked Torie.

Glen thought for a moment. "Possibly. If whoever did this was caring for her, washing her, moving her around. Maybe."

"What kind of monster would do this?" demanded Jasmin. "I mean, it couldn't have been the mayor, right? He was a good man."

"Or so we thought," said Glen.

"Maybe this town didn't know him as well as you think. Good men can do very bad things when no one is watching them. You said yourself that he pretty much kept to himself, that no one knew much about his personal life."

"Yes, that's true," said Jasmin. "But this…" She waved her hand at the space around her. "Someone would have to be clearly unwell to do this. Plus, where did the magic binding come from? That was some serious mojo locking her in place."

"And that's why I don't think we should leave her alone," said Torie. She had been thinking about Max's request and found herself agreeing with the wolf. "Glen, what will happen to her if she goes to the hospital?"

"Well, more likely than not she will be turned over to

the state and placed in a geriatric care facility. They will do a search for any next of kin; but if Max can't turn anything up on her, there is no reason to think the state system will."

Torie frowned and looked back at the woman. "I can't stand the thought of her being in one of those places. No. She will come stay with me until we can figure this out. Can you help with her care until she's healed?"

"Of course," said Glen. "Glad to. I'll go grab some supplies from the hospital and meet you back at your place tonight."

"Good. I've already called Elric and asked him to move some of the extra furniture from my guest house into your house," said Jasmin. "At least that way, you will both have a bedroom set up while you wait for your delivery in a couple of days." She saw the way Torie was looking at her. "What? Oh please, like there was ever a chance you were going to let her go anywhere else. I know you, Torie Bliss."

Torie laughed. "Yes. Yes you do."

Max had wrapped the old woman in a blanket and carried her gently down the stairs where they placed her in the back of Glen's first responder wagon. They made their way to Torie's new home, and Max lifted her out of the vehicle and headed for Torie's large, double-door entry.

"I'm going to run up to my place and get some nourishing herbs that will help her heal," said Jasmin, leaning out of her driver's side window before easing her car back onto the main road and heading for her home.

Torie waved after her and then turned to head back into her home. One of the things she had been sure to build with her new house was a sizable greenhouse in which she would be able to grow her own supplemental herbs and plants. Like the rest of the house, it wasn't ready just yet, and she cursed herself for having been so slow in getting everything in place.

Elric opened the doors and met them on the porch.

"Everything is set. I moved the furniture from Jasmin's guest house into the main and secondary bedrooms on the main floor. I figured she would not be in any condition to tackle the stairs daily."

"Perfect," said Torie, leaning forward to give him a quick peck on the lips. "I can't thank you enough for doing this."

"Hey, it's what I'm here for," he said.

"Really?" said Max. "A powerful werewolf, one of the most feared enforcers in all of Trinity Cove, and now you're a furniture mover."

Torie rolled her eyes at Max's jab. She knew deep down he was happy for his old beta, but she wished that sometimes he would curb the jabs he threw Elric's way. For his part, Elric just smiled and shook it off.

"I think we are both a lot better off now than when we were in Trinity. You don't fool me; I can tell you're loving your new role as peacekeeper."

Max didn't respond, just shouldered his way past him into the large entry of the home. Effie began to moan, twisting in his arms.

"What is it? What's happening?" Torie asked.

"I don't know. She was out cold and now, she's getting agitated again," replied Max.

Glen rushed to his side to examine the woman. "Get her into the bedroom. Something isn't right."

Max followed Torie as she led them down a back hall to the space that Elric had set up for them. For a guest room it was spacious with a large window looking out over the graceful, sloping back yard. A set of French doors led to a private deck as well.

Max placed her on the bed that had been positioned to take in the views and stepped back so that Glen could examine her.

The nurse checked her vitals and breathing.

"Her heart rate is increasing, and she seems to be having trouble breathing. But there isn't anything that should be causing this."

Torie looked on in panic as the old woman struggled to draw breath, watching as Glen feverishly dug into her bag for any meds that she felt might help the situation.

"It's almost as if she is having a reaction to something," said Glen. "But we haven't given her anything." She glanced quickly about the room. "There are no flowers in here, nothing heavily scented that she could be reacting to; I don't get it."

Torie's eyes lit up. Had it not been so comical she would have smacked herself in the forehead for having a V8 moment.

"Of course, why didn't I consider it? The magic that bound her. There may be some residual traces of it clinging to her. It could be reacting to the wards built into the home. Let me see if I can temporarily drop them, see if it makes a difference."

She stood and closed her eyes, stretching her mind out to feel for the mystical barriers she and Jasmin had erected. Waving her hand, she pulled them down, letting them go slack for the moment.

Almost at once the older woman began to settle back down. Her eyes fluttered open for a moment and a slight smile crossed her lips as her breathing returned to normal.

"Okay, well, whatever you just did seems to have done the trick," said Glen. "I'm going to go get some meds for her and some bandages and salves to help with those bedsores. I'll be back in an hour. Call me immediately if anything changes with her."

"I'm heading out too," said Max. "I need to start chasing down any leads as to who this woman is and what her connection to our dead mayor is."

Effie's eyes flew open. "What did you say? Did someone just say my son is dead?"

Grief racked her voice as she began to cry, her tiny body contorting as emotion took her over. "Oh God no...please tell me it's not true. He can't be dead. He's all I have. Who will take care of me now?"

Torie moved to comfort her, shooting Max an irritated look. Glen moved to her bag, taking out a small bottle and a syringe. The thought of giving the woman a full sedative, without the proper equipment to monitor her was not something she relished, but she could also see that Effie's grief was causing her considerable pain and stress. She pushed the small needle into the IV in the woman's arm and gave it a small push. The dose was not even enough to harm a child, but she hoped it would have a calming effect on the poor lady.

It worked, and she started to relax, her body growing limp in Torie's arms. Torie eased her back onto the pillows and stroked her hair, pushing a stray strand off her face.

"Well, that was not how she should have found out," she said, giving Max another dose of side eye. "But we will deal with that later. How long will she sleep?"

"With that dose, maybe just an hour. You'll have to be ready to address this with her when she wakes up," said Glen.

That wasn't all Torie had to address.

Why was there still magic in her system? The spell she and Jasmin had performed should have removed all traces from her. Maybe the answer to that would help them figure out just what was going on here.

Chapter Six

Torie stood in her new kitchen, taking it all in as the last of the furniture had finally been delivered. Cooking had always been one of her passions. The one activity that never failed to bring her peace.

Even when she would have been considered wealthy, she always prepared dinner for her family. Her ex-husband could never understand why she didn't let the "help" do the cooking. He never understood that the kitchen was her refuge; the one place where she had complete control over what came in and out of her space. There were no expectations; no pressure to perform; no criticism. Well, except for her own self-criticism at the roast not turning out perfectly or the soufflé not rising just so.

And she was working on that as well. In this, her second start in life, she was determined to be kinder to herself; to give herself grace in all areas of her life, not just the kitchen.

For better or worse she had pretty much designed every aspect of the house herself, right down to the finishes and the soothing light gray paint colors that could be found throughout. The kitchen had been her focal point throughout the build, however.

She had picked out a beautiful white quartz with just a touch of blue-gray veining running through it for the counter tops and the massive center island. The island was a single piece that had taken workers the better part of a day to move in and install. The waterfall design would be time-less over the blue cabinetry. She had gone with white cabi-nets for the rest of the kitchen, pairing it with a white and blue glass backsplash.

All of it was set off by the pewter hardware on the drawers and cabinet doors that perfectly played off the custom pewter appliances. A large, commercial refrigerator and a massive eight-burner high-end range added just the right amount of bling to her design.

She had also installed a double wall oven, customized to her height. Her knees were not what they once were, and they loved to remind her of that at every Thanksgiving when she bent over to haul a twenty-pound turkey out of the oven.

"Why do you always cook such a large bird when there is only the three of us?" her husband would ask. Always with that tone. It wasn't menacing or mocking. Just judg-mental with a side dish of disappointment.

Why hadn't she seen him for what he really was sooner?

What she had secretly always hoped was that someone; family, friends, co-workers, would announce that they suddenly found themselves without a place to go for Thanksgiving and she would be able to open her home to them last minute. Assuring them it was no problem, and indeed it wouldn't be because she always made sure there would be more than enough for everyone.

But that never happened.

Now that she was in a place to do so, however, she could fulfill that secret hope she carried. With a kitchen like this, she could feed a small army.

Heck, she might even be capable of coming up with something to win the chocolate competition this year at the festival. If she decided to enter it, which she had still been debating.

The kitchen, combined with the dedicated dining space, could easily seat up to fifteen people. She would make sure that holidays would be festive for all her new friends.

No, that wasn't right. If she had learned anything since moving to Singing Falls, it was that these people had become her family. When someone saves your life, and vice versa, you tend to move a little beyond the friend stage.

She walked through the kitchen to large glass doors that led to the expansive patio and decking that overlooked the backyard. Because the house was built on a lot with a severe slope to the back, one that dove downward at a forty-five-degree angle before hitting the old growth trees, she had to have a massive retaining wall built to create a level backyard.

It had been worth the extra money as there was now room in the back not only for her greenhouse, but also for a fire pit, built-in custom grill area that included a stone pizza oven, and a second seating area under the impressive foliage that rose all around her. Building up the backyard had the effect of bringing the space up into the middle of the trees. She had contemplated installing a pool as well but knew it would be a nightmare to maintain because of the constant falling leaves. Plus, she didn't swim and wasn't particularly fond of being in water.

She walked to the edge of the yard where an impressive

five-foot iron railing rose to keep anyone from stumbling over the edge of the retaining wall, and just as importantly, keep anyone outside the property from getting in.

If they could scale that retaining wall and make it over the railing, they would have to be a *Spiderman*. Or a were-wolf. Or a vampire. Or…she cut that train of thought off. There were probably any number of supernaturals in Singing Falls who would have no problem getting to her house if they wanted to.

Hence the array of wards she and Jasmin had created. Getting onto the grounds was one thing; making it into the house was something else altogether.

She made her way back inside, through the kitchen, and into the open great room. She smiled at her new furnishings. The sheer size of the room had demanded large pieces, but she had made sure they were comfortable. Couches that invited one to nap on but weren't so deep that they were difficult to get out of. Large, modern wingback-style chairs that flanked the massive fireplace just begged for someone to crash into them with a good book.

She had also made sure there were plenty of options in the space for her to put a large Christmas tree up come holiday time. High ceilings had been a must and that meant she could set up the tallest one she could drag in. Actually, the tallest one that Elric could drag in. What was the point in having a boyfriend with super strength if it wasn't used to move furniture and lug things about?

Boyfriend.

It was something she had only recently allowed herself to think of Elric as. She had taken her fair share of ribbing from Jasmin and Fionna the first time that word had slipped her lips in conversation. Truthfully, she wasn't entirely comfortable with the word itself. It seemed like something out of place for a woman of her age, but what else was there? Man-friend? Lover…the very thought of saying that made her shiver in disgust. Until something better came along, boyfriend it would be. The term had become part of her inner and outer vernacular when she referred to the wolf. He had become a part of her and as natural to her as breathing.

While she wasn't sure where things were headed with him, she knew she did not want to rush into anything. He hadn't asked about moving in, and she had been careful not to raise the subject. That was inevitably where things were headed, but Torie knew it would have to feel right for both of them if and when that time came.

Also, there was the matter of what to do with her new houseguest as well.

Her watch buzzed, reminding her that it was time for Effie to take her next dose of medication.

She made her way down the back hall from the great room to the guest suite and knocked on the door.

"Come in, Torie," came a voice from the other side.

Torie eased the door open and stepped inside.

Effie was sitting in a recliner next to the large windows overlooking the back yard. She turned her head slightly in Torie's direction as she approached.

"Effie, it's time for you to take another antibiotic. You're almost finished with this round."

Glen had been concerned about the nasty bedsores she had on her backside, one of which seemed to be festering, so she had suggested the elderly woman take some antibiotics just in case.

"How are you feeling?" Torie asked as she moved to the nightstand, opened the pill bottle and poured a cup of water from a plastic pitcher.

"I'm feeling much better, thank you. I am starting to get some of my strength back I believe."

She was indeed improving. The progress she was making was incredible. The pressure points were healing at a remarkable rate, and while her frame was still slight and her musculature almost non-existent, she had bounced back physically far quicker than Glen, or any of them, had expected. The fact that she was able to get up out of her bed and make her way to the recliner without aide was impressive; although it still made Torie very nervous.

"You know, I am more than happy to help you to the chair from bed, Effie. You shouldn't be up and about yet."

The older woman waved her hand dismissively in Torie's direction.

"Pssh," she said. "I will not be a burden to anyone, least of all someone who has so kindly opened their home to me."

She reached out her hands as Torie approached to give her the cup of water and the pill. She tossed it back and drank the entire cup before handing it back to Torie.

"Speaking of homes, when can I return to mine?"

Torie didn't answer right away. Truth was, she did not know when Effie could return home. The house had been thoroughly investigated by the forensic team looking for any clues that could help with solving the mayor's death.

The autopsy on him had revealed that he had a heart attack, but because of his age and apparent good health, as well as his standing as a public figure, an official investigation had been launched. The fact that his own mother had been found with all signs pointing to her being a victim of elder abuse, had also waved several red flags in Max's eyes.

The mayor's home wasn't officially a crime scene, but it

also wasn't some place they would allow Effie to return to just yet.

"If you're worried about me, don't be," she said. "I lived alone in that house for many years. I'll be fine. Besides, Terry will be there to take care of me. I just hope he doesn't lock me in my room again."

Her small voice trailed off, and Torie could see memories flooding her face.

"Oh. That's right. Terry won't be there again, will he?" Sadness crossed her features as she turned her face back towards the window. "You know I love being in this spot right here. This time of day, I can feel the sun on my face, and it feels so warm."

Torie smiled as she moved to sit in a chair on the other side of the window.

"Effie, do you remember anything about what led you to be in your room like that? Why would your son keep you in there?"

So far, the woman had not been able to tell them anything about what led to her restraint on the bed. Torie and Jasmin had hinted at magic or witchcraft, but the old woman had not taken the bait. Either she had no idea about the supernatural or she truly had no memory of being bound to her bed.

Although her mind had started to heal just as quickly as her body, she had pretty much blocked whatever happened inside the house involving her son. All she remembered was being confined to her room, but not the bed.

She shook her head slowly to Torie's inquiry.

"I'm sorry, but like I said, Terry said it was for my own good to stay in my bedroom while he was out running errands or conducting business. He was always going on about being afraid I might fall.

"But I've never fallen once in that house. I know it like the back of my hand. I kept telling him that, but he wouldn't listen, always making sure I stayed in my room unless he was in the house as well. He never listens to me... *listened*, I mean."

Torie didn't answer, instead she turned her gaze to the window as well. "The deck is nearly complete. I can't wait to take you outside; the weather is going to be perfect over the next couple of days."

Effie sniffled as her gray eyes began to water.

"Effie, what is it?" asked Torie.

"I...I haven't been outside in longer than I can remember. I didn't realize how much I missed it until you mentioned it to me."

Torie started to speak but was interrupted by another knock on the bedroom door. It pushed open, and Elric stuck his head inside.

"Elric," said Torie. "I didn't hear you come in."

"Sorry, I just pulled up." He had a look on his face that told Torie something wasn't quite right. "Um, Torie, can you come outside for a minute. There's something I think you need to see."

"Of course." She stood up and started towards him, but then turned back to Effie. "I'll be back in a few. And don't you worry. We are going to spend as much time outside as you want."

She smiled and left the room, following Elric as he hurried towards the main entrance.

"Elric, what on earth is it? You're in an awful hurry."

He didn't slow down until he reached the large doors that opened onto the front porch. He placed a hand on the handle, but before opening the door, he gave Torie a long look that she could not read.

"It appears someone has left you a gift."

He opened the door to reveal a large, rough, woven basket with a yellow and green cotton blanket inside.

Torie stared, not quite sure what to make of it. She leaned closer, only to see the blanket move slightly. She nearly jumped back, one hand on Elric's arm as she regarded the now wiggling basket.

"What in the world?" she asked.

Elric took a deep breath and bent down, lifting the blanket away.

Torie's gasp was audible as she covered her mouth with a hand.

"Is that…?" she started.

Elric could only nod, not taking his eyes off the basket.

"Yep," he said. "That…is a dragon. A baby dragon, to be exact."

Chapter Seven

Torie, Jasmin and Fionna stood together in the great room looking down at the little beast that lay peacefully on the floor. It was rolling around in a ball, trying desperately to get its own tail into its mouth.

"Where on earth did this come from?" asked Jasmin in dismay.

"Like I said…no idea," said Torie. "It just turned up on my steps, literally."

"There was no scent around it," said Elric. "If another person or animal dropped it off, I can't track them."

"This is literally the cutest thing I have ever seen in my life!" exclaimed Fionna as she squatted down to extend a finger towards the dragon.

The little dragon momentarily forgot about his tail and grasped at the tip of her finger with his own tiny claws, much as a baby would when presented with an adult's digit.

It was roughly eight inches long from tip of its horned snout to the end of a spiked tail. Tiny, veined wings sprouted from its chubby little sides, and shimmered in the light. The creature was purple with silver tiger stripes along its scaled body. It had four little legs, the front two slightly shorter than the back ones, that ended in tiny, nearly iridescent claws. There was a ridge of tough, silver hair-like projections that ran from the top of its head down its back, terminating mid-tail.

Fionna held out her hand and the dragon marched onto her palm, curling its tail around itself as she raised it to eye level. The creature's eyes were two orbs the color of emeralds. They tracked her face, moving from her to the rest of the faces staring at it. When it locked on Torie's features, it rose onto its hind legs and flapped tiny wings excitedly before settling back down into a little ball.

"Um, so dragons are a thing, huh?" said Torie.

"Honestly, I assumed they probably existed, but I've never actually seen one. Or heard of anyone who has seen one," said Jasmin. "Fionna, Elric, are either of you familiar with these?"

The wolf shook his head. "I reached out to Max and he has no knowledge about them either."

"Well, it stands to reason they exist," said Fionna. "My grammy used to tell stories about them. She said they are part of our supernatural spectrum and that they are shifters just like the rest of us. But we always thought that was just a tale she told us to keep us from roaming too far out into the woods when we were young. She always said dragons ate other shifters."

"Shifters, huh?" said Torie. "Then maybe I can talk to it."

Jasmin shrugged. "Worth a try, I guess."

Torie leaned in, smiling at the little creature. Instantly, it rose onto its hind legs again and peered deeply into Torie's eyes.

"Hello there, little one. Aren't you just the cutest little dragon ever? Can you tell me your name?"

She listened carefully, tapping into that part of her hex power that allowed her to communicate with shifters in their animal form. It was the first of her magical abilities that had manifested and had remained one of her most primal abilities. One that came so naturally to her.

The dragon studied her, moving its head from side to side. Then, slowly and deliberately, it raised its tiny paws in her direction.

Torie reached out a hand and the dragon happily skittered from Fionna's palm to Torie's hand. It raced up her arm, far faster and agile than its chunky form should have allowed, until it came to rest on her shoulder, making itself at home with a patch of her hair cascading in front of it.

"Oh! Well, okay then," said Torie.

"What did it say?" asked Jasmin.

"Not a thing. I can't hear anything coming from it. Not even a hint of a whisper," said Torie as she reached up with her finger to playfully tickle the dragon's stomach.

"Well, one thing's for sure," said Fionna, "it knows you."

"Well, what am I going to do with a dragon?" answered Torie. "And a baby one at that. What do they eat? Is it house broken? I don't have a clue what to do with it."

"I'll take it if you don't want it," said Fionna, quickly.

"You most certainly will not," said Jasmin. "I may never have seen one, but dragons are most certainly magical creatures. And if one appeared here then it is for a reason. The fact that it seems so taken with Torie means something. We just don't know what."

Fionna's eyes lit up and she practically jumped up and

down. "Oh! What if it is your familiar? Jasmin, didn't your sister say—" She froze, her words cut off by the look Jasmin threw her. "Didn't that woman-who-shall-not-be-named, say that all witches should have a familiar at some point?"

Torie didn't answer, her lower lip twisting to one side as she chewed on it.

"I suppose that could be true," she said. "But that really doesn't make sense since Jasmin doesn't have one, and she's way more experienced with this stuff than I am."

"Is that a dig at my age?" Jasmin replied, narrowing her eyes.

"Not at all," said Torie. "Okay, well, maybe a small one."

"Hmph. Well, at least my hair hasn't turned gray."

"Ouch. That hurt," said Torie as she reached up to run a finger along the silver streak that had developed and ran through the center of her hair. It happened in her last encounter with the hunter and Jasmin's sister. No matter what she had tried, there was no getting rid of it. She could dye it at night and would wake up with it silver again the next morning. Even magic had failed to reverse it. Now, she just accepted and lived with it. If anything, it was starting to grow on her.

"I think it's incredibly sexy," said Elric, stepping in to turn the conversation back to the focus at hand, "but we still need to figure out what to do with your little friend here."

"Well, I say for the time being, it obviously has to stay here with Torie," said Fionna. "It's not like we can just walk it deep into the woods and set it free. It may be a dragon, but it's still a baby."

"Fionna is right," said Jasmin. "There is something weird going on around here. First the mayor ends up dead, then we find his mother magically chained to a bed, and now a dragon shows up out of nowhere?"

"Don't forget the festival," added Fionna, arching both eyebrows when everyone turned to look at her. "What? It's an important part of the town history, and we can't have Torie distracted if she's going to win the chocolate contest."

Torie held up a single finger. "I never said I was entering that."

"Oh you will," said Fionna. "And even if you don't, you still have to be the main judge. Especially now that the mayor can't preside. The town is in a panic thinking that the festival might get cancelled this year. That has never happened."

The fact that the town was more worried about a festival not happening than they were over the death of a public figure surprised Torie. But unlike her and her friends, the town had no clue the mayor may have been involved in something dark and mystical that might have contributed to his death.

Also, the mayor wasn't carrying the name and contact information of anyone else in the town either. So there was that to consider.

"Alright it's solved then," said Jasmin. "I'm going to go to the library and see what I can dig up on dragons. Fionna, you go to the civic center and let everyone know that the festival will continue, and that Sheriff Max is working to find a temporary chair of the committee until the mayor's successor can be named."

"You know, there is such a thing as the internet," said Fionna. "I'm sure it's much more thorough than a library."

"Not this town's library," replied Jasmin. "There are old tomes here that will have information not found on the internet."

"And what about me?" asked Torie.

"You have your hands full here. Between taking care of Effie and a baby dragon, your life just got hella busy. Plus planning and hosting a birthday party."

"Oh no, that isn't important in light of things," said Fionna.

"Nope. That one is not even up for debate. It is important, and it will still happen. End of discussion," said Torie.

"Well, if you insist. Also, don't forget you have to come up with a winning chocolate recipe," added Fionna as she headed for the door.

Torie just rolled her eyes and turned to Elric. "And you? Are you leaving me to deal with all of this too?"

"Never. Well, maybe just for a bit. I need to find Max. We may know someone who knows a thing or two about dragons. But I'd rather not say who until we find out if he'll help." He gave her a quick peck and headed out the door with Fionna.

Jasmin looked at Torie. "Call me if you need something. But you might want to take that thing outside to see if it needs to do its business. And figure out if it needs something to eat. And maybe keep it away from the gas lines…you know, just in case it can work up a spark or something."

Torie's eyes grew wide. "Do you think it can breathe fire? Oh dear. I've never even owned a pet before, let alone one that can breathe fire. Maybe this isn't a good idea."

"It will be fine, Torie. You raised a baby. Just think of it as a four-legged baby."

Torie wrinkled her nose up at the thought of that and it made Jasmin laugh hard.

"I'll be back after the library. Have fun."

And with that, she was out the door, leaving Torie alone

with a tiny dragon perched on her shoulder and an elderly blind woman in her guest room.

She felt a tug at her hair and realized the dragon was trying to eat a strand of it.

"No you don't," she said, reaching up to remove it from her shoulder.

She carried it into the kitchen and placed it on the island where it stared up at her intently with those dark, green eyes.

"I suppose I should feed you," she said. "I don't suppose you can tell me what you like?"

She only half expected an answer, but when none was forthcoming, she moved over to the refrigerator and opened the large door to peer inside. She hadn't had a chance to do any proper shopping to stock up, but there were some staples that she had managed to pick up.

"Well, the obvious choice is this," she said to herself as she withdrew a carton of milk. She went to a cabinet and retrieved a small saucer. Placing it on the island she poured a little milk into it and slid it in front of the dragon.

It looked at the milk then back up at Torie, not quite sure what to do.

"Like this." Torie bent over the cabinet and pretended to drink from the saucer. "Now you do it." She motioned from the dragon to the saucer.

Tentatively, the tiny dragon dropped to all fours and cautiously made its way to the milk. It leaned in, sniffed at it, and then once again looked up at Torie.

"Go on," she whispered. "It's good for you."

Again, the dragon leaned over the saucer and eyed the milk. Slowly, it dipped its snout into the milk and took a cautious sip.

Immediately, it sat up and spat it out in disgust, giving a little sneeze at the same time.

"So much for that, huh."

Torie returned to the fridge and tried orange juice, placing it on another saucer, only to receive the same rejection as before.

"Okay, so maybe unlike babies, you don't do liquids."

She looked around and her eyes settled on a bowl of fruit that was on one of the countertops. She took an apple and grabbed a banana that was hanging from a hook and took them to the island. Peeling the apple and cutting it into slices she placed one in front of the dragon and then did the same with the banana before crossing her arms and stepping back to watch what would happen.

The dragon bent down to sniff at the fruit before using its little paws to push it away. Then it sat up and again looked intently at Torie.

"Okay, I don't know what else to try," she said. "There's nothing else here, and I have no clue what a baby dragon eats. Unless..."

She returned to the refrigerator and peered inside, reaching to pull out one of the drawers. Inside she found a packet of hamburgers she had picked up. She and Elric were going to break in the new grill when it was ready by making some good ole burgers for dinner one evening.

She dropped it onto the island and slowly broke the tape securing the paper around the meat. As soon as the packet was unwrapped, the little dragon perked up, standing on its hind legs as it sniffed the air.

"Well, that certainly seems to have gotten your attention."

Torie tore a chunk of the raw meat free and placed it on a paper towel in front of it. Immediately the dragon was on it, biting into the soft meat and swallowing chunks. In no time the towel was cleaned, and it looked up at her expectantly.

"Alright. A little more, but until I find out more about you and your digestive system, let's not overdo it."

She tore off a bigger chunk of meat, plopped it down, and watched in glee as it met the same fate as the previous piece.

Once the dragon finished, she put the rest back into the fridge, despite the longing look the dragon gave her.

"That's enough of that, little dragon. I suppose I now have to watch you for signs that you need to go. Or do I just walk you? It would be a lot more helpful if you could just speak to me like other supernatural creatures."

She extended her hand and let the little creature scamper up her arm to again perch on her shoulder.

"Plus, I suppose I should come up with a name for you. I can't just keep calling you dragon."

She thought about it, trying to decide what an appropriate name for such a cute little beast would be. She had no idea if it was male or female, so something gender neutral would be in order.

Her thought process was interrupted by a clamor that came from the back of the house.

Effie.

Without thinking, she hurried to the guest room to find the elderly woman on all fours, desperately feeling around to collect pieces of a broken table lamp that had hit the floor.

"Oh, Torie, I am so sorry," she exclaimed. "I'm still not used to where everything is in this room and clumsy old me broke your light I believe."

"Effie, don't worry about it. I'll clean that up. Let me help you—"

Before she could take a few steps forward and bend down to help the woman up, she felt a rustling on her shoulder. The dragon rattled its tail in a way that made Torie's hair fly about as it leaned forward and issued a deep hiss at Effie.

Then, with no forewarning at all, the little creature leapt off Torie's shoulder and raced across the floor at the blind woman.

Chapter Eight

Torie shrieked, and scampered after it, throwing herself onto the floor in her attempts to reach the flurry of tiny claws and fangs. She managed to grab it by the tail just as it was about to reach Effie.

She hauled the struggling dragon back and held it tightly as it twisted and squirmed, hissing all the time.

"Oh my, Torie. Is that your cat making such a fuss?" asked Effie.

"Oh, um, yes, it sure is. It's still getting used to the new house. Let me just put it outside the door and then I'll help you. Just don't move."

Torie stood and rushed over to the door, setting the dragon down just outside in the hallway. She held up a single finger, getting its attention.

"That is no!" she said sternly. "You understand? No." She pointed to the room where Effie was staying. "You wait here, I'll be back in a moment."

The dragon didn't move but instead was focused on

Torie. She squinted, looking closer as something caught her eye.

Was that...smoke! Little wisps were coming from the dragon's nostrils as it huffed, focusing intently on the space behind Torie.

Again, she shook her finger at the dragon and backed up until she was in the bedroom and gently closed the door after her.

"Okay," she said, using one hand to brush her hair back in place. "Let me help you up."

She carefully took Effie by the arm and guided her to her feet. She led the woman back to her bed and helped her to lie back before walking around to the lamp and picking up the pieces. Luckily, it hadn't shattered, but only cracked into a couple of large pieces that were easy enough to gather and put in the wastepaper basket.

"I am so sorry," said Effie.

"Don't be. I wasn't sure about that light anyway. Now I have a reason to get a new one."

"I...I hate being such a bother to you, Torie. I feel like I'm just taking up your space here."

"Not at all. I like having you here. It's nice having someone else to talk to."

As she said it, she realized she truly meant it. It was amazing having Elric around, and she certainly never tired of Fionna and Jasmin; but there was something different about having the elderly woman to care for.

She reached out and pushed a stray strand of gray away from Effie's face. "How are you feeling? You seem to be moving around much better."

"Except for when I'm knocking stuff over," Effie quipped. "But I feel much better. Not as sore. And I think those spots on my back are all gone now. Thanks to that nice lady doctor and her creams."

Torie laughed. She couldn't wait to tell Glen she had been elevated to the role of doctor. She would definitely get a kick out of that.

"Well, I'm glad to see you're feeling better. Tonight, why don't we plan to have some dinner out on the patio? Everything should be ready by then. I'll have Elric pick us up something special to break in the new outdoor area. Is there anything in particular you would like? Any allergies?"

The old woman smiled, her face seeming to light up.

"Oh, I'm not very particular; I can eat just about anything. But you know what would be really good? Some kind of meat. Red meat if possible. My son would never let me eat red meat. He said it was bad for my health."

Torie smiled. "Red meat it is then. Try to get some rest and I'll be back in a couple of hours for your next dose of antibiotics. If you need anything, just call out."

She left the room, carefully pulling it closed behind her. Then, worried that she wouldn't be able to hear Effie if she called out, she decided to leave the door cracked open. She frowned, making a mental note to always be aware of where the dragon was just in case it decided to venture back toward the room later.

The dragon wasn't in the hall where she had left it, so she headed back towards the main living area, giving little whistles as she went, hoping the dragon would respond just as any other pet might.

She found it perched on the island, curled into a little ball. At her approach, it unfurled itself and gave her its full attention. Casting a sly look from the refrigerator back to Torie, it sniffed the air, a dark red tongue snaking out to lick at its chops.

"No, I don't think you need any more food right now. Were you huffing smoke back there? Are you a little fire-breather? And how did you get up onto this island?"

She looked around. The island was more than waist high for her and the chairs that were made for it had not been placed along the back side yet. Were baby dragons able to fly? Its little wings didn't seem capable of supporting the creature, but who knows?

All of that aside, she was more concerned about the behavior it exhibited towards Effie. The way it charged at her had taken Torie by surprise. It hadn't shown any aggression around her friends and had seemed nothing but loving towards Torie.

Maybe, since it was a supernatural creature itself, it sensed some form of kinship with the shifters around it. With Effie being human, the dragon had responded completely differently. What if it had never seen a human before? Would it perceive it as a threat?

"Well, we can't have that," said Torie, reaching out to playfully tickle it. "Also, I really do need a name for you. Hmmm, maybe there is a way that you can tell me a little more about yourself. Hold still, don't move."

She extended her finger and placed it lightly on the dragon's head and closed her eyes.

"Spirits of magic, strong and kind,
let me see inside this creature's mind."

Instantly, images flooded into Torie's mind. It was like a kaleidoscope of images that flashed and swirled too quickly for her to decipher. The one image that she did see, the one that seemed to dominate everything, was that of hunger and blood accompanied by bones snapping and flesh being torn.

Torie jumped back, her head aching at the sudden onslaught of images.

She stared at the little dragon, not quite sure of what to think. Were those memories? No, they couldn't have been. The dragon was too small to cause the carnage that she had seen. Perhaps they were images of something the dragon had seen. That seemed more likely. Either way, it was a behavior that she wasn't going to risk happening with this little guy, especially not after seeing his reaction to Effie.

Especially not in a town filled with humans.

An idea came to her, one that she knew she should run by Jasmin first. But Jasmin was busy at the moment, and hadn't she been telling Torie more and more to trust her instincts? Well, Torie's instincts were telling her to do what she was about to do. If this was her familiar, then that meant she was responsible for its behavior. She smiled at the dragon and gave it a nod.

> *"Hear my plea and do my will,*
> *let this creature of myth's mind be still,*
> *though you're strong in claw and fang,*
> *I bind you from harming any human thing."*

The dragon seemed to flinch as it stared at Torie for just a second, before once again resuming staring at the refrigerator and then back at Torie longingly.

"Okay, maybe just a little bit more, but then I'm taking you outside to hopefully do your business."

She studied the creature as it gleefully choked down more raw meat, oblivious to her and the world around it. It really was like a puppy, she thought, the way the world would cease to exist around them when it came time to eat. The dragon's tail even waved happily back and forth as it fed.

"I think I am going to call you Leo." She wasn't sure why that name had suddenly popped into her head, but she was pretty sure it worked for the dragon. She was also certain the dragon was a male, though she wasn't sure how she knew that either.

"Leo the dragon. I like that. Okay, Leo, enough food for today. Hopefully my friends will have some luck finding more information about you. But in the meantime," she picked Leo up and perched him on her shoulder, "let's go walk you and see what happens."

As it turned out, it was a very productive walk.

Torie had never really owned a pet so she certainly had no need for a leash and collar. She had briefly wondered how that would even work with a baby dragon; eventually deciding against it. Turned out, she didn't need to bother worrying about it at all. Little Leo was intent on her every move and stayed very close to her; when she stepped he stepped, when she stopped, he stopped.

"Go on now, go do your business," she chided. "Isn't there a children's show about how to train your dragon, or something like that? I wonder if there is one called how to housebreak your dragon. Now that's what they should focus on." She was mostly talking to herself and only partially to the dragon. He sat on the ground staring up at her intently, head cocked to one side as if he were trying to decipher her words.

She moved to a small clearing on the other side of the freshly paved driveway and waited, staring at the dragon.

"Okay, let's try something else."

She bent over and looked deeply into his eyes, creating a

mental image of what she wanted him to do, and then, very firmly stated, "Go potty."

To her surprise, he immediately did just that. Moving away from her just far enough to comfortably go to the bathroom before gleefully hopping back over to sit at her feet, patiently waiting for her next command.

"Well, that was easy." She looked over at what he had left on her lawn and wrinkled her nose. "And I think I just found yet another job for Elric to do. Come on, Leo, let's get back inside."

She checked her watch, wondering when her friends would be returning with news of some kind. In the meantime, she had things that required her immediate attention.

First, was creating a to-do list for Fionna's birthday party. The thought of that made her light up. If there was one thing she had always been great at, it was throwing parties. The minute it was suggested that she host, she had started creating a running list in the back of her mind of everything she needed to make this a truly standout occasion.

The other thing she needed to do was start thinking about what she was going to create for entry in the chocolate competition. Granted, she had not been thrilled about it, but she could see how important it was to continue the tradition her mother had always been a part of, so she wanted to make sure that she represented by bringing her A-game. No chocolate cake or pan of brownies for her. No. She needed something different and new.

Entering the house, she made her way to her study, which was on the opposite side of the house from the guest suite where Effie was resting. She was tempted to check in on the older woman but thought better of it when she remembered the way Leo had reacted to her.

"That's another thing for the list," she said, looking down at Leo as they walked into her study. "Finding out what to keep you in while we figure out what to do with you."

She briefly thought of purchasing a dog crate for him, but immediately cast that thought aside. She couldn't bear the mental image of him locked in a crate, looking up at her with what she could only assume would be enormous, sad green eyes; possibly with a single tear running down his little snout.

No. No crates.

So that left creating a space inside a room for him.

She looked around at her study, and it hit her that this could very well be that space. The floors were a beautiful gray vinyl that would stand up to his little claws, and there was a wall of windows that faced the woods to the side of her house. There would be plenty of natural light for the little guy, and more than enough space for him to roam around in when she was not home.

She moved to the desk that sat on one side of the room, flanked by floor-to-ceiling bookcases. Taking a seat, she took out a leather-bound notepad and pen and started creating her list. A flurry of movement caught her eye as Leo effortlessly leapt onto the desktop to see what she was doing.

"Well, that explains how you got onto the kitchen island," she said, reaching out to scratch his back with one of her fingers. "And here I thought you could fly."

She was deep in thought, working on the guest list for Fionna's party when her cell phone chimed. It was a text from Elric. He had found someone who knew a lot about dragons.

Torie picked up the phone and dialed his number.

"That is great," she said. "Do I need to go to him? Should I bring Leo…oh yeah, that's what I've named him."

"Ummm, that sounds like a great name for a dragon, but I think it would be a lot easier if I bring this guy to you. If you're okay with that?"

"Of course I am. Why wouldn't I be? You sound weird, what's wrong?"

"Nothing's wrong. It's just…the guy that Max and I know who is knowledgeable about these things, lives down in Trinity Cove. And, well, you'll definitely need to be home when we arrive. You'll have to…how should I put this… invite him in. And you'll definitely need to allow him to pass through your wards. And I have to wait for the sun to go down to pick him up."

Torie didn't say anything at first.

"I see. Well, I trust you. So, if you think this is the best way, I'll be here when you get back."

She hung up the call and sat back in her chair, releasing a deep sigh.

Trinity Cove was the sister town to the south of Singing Falls. Like Singing Falls, it too was known to be a haven for the supernatural. Only, Trinity Cove's supernatural population was more of the darker variety of beings. Ones that you really didn't want to cross paths with.

The kind that liked to go bump in the night.

And going by what Elric said, there was only one kind of supernatural that needed to be invited in and would only come to visit after dark.

Vampire.

Chapter Nine

Torie left Leo in the study while she checked in on Effie. The older woman was napping peacefully as Torie adjusted the blanket up around her a little and then quietly shut the door as she backed out of the room. Then, retrieving Leo, she headed into the kitchen to put on a kettle of water for some tea. She had reached out to Jasmin and Fionna to let them know what Elric had relayed to her. To no surprise, both had stated they were dropping what they were doing and were heading right over.

Truthfully, it made her feel better, knowing they were going to be at her side when a vampire crossed the threshold of her home. The only experience she had with vampires since moving to Singing Falls had been with Arnold, the town lawyer and accountant who maintained the trust from which she withdrew the financial means to make everything around her possible.

Arnold had fallen under the control of a manipulative warlock and had attacked Torie and her friends, resulting in his death. It had not been a pleasant experience at all, and she was not looking forward to meeting another of his kind.

Vampires were not looked kindly on in Singing Falls. But neither were werewolves at one time, she reminded herself. She at least owed it to Elric to welcome this…man, graciously. She trusted Elric and knew that he would never willingly place her in danger.

If he trusted a vampire enough to bring him into her home, then she would trust him as well. At least until he gave her reason not to.

And if that happened, she was again thankful that she had her hex powers back; and if that wasn't enough, she knew Fionna would be packing at least one stake.

Torie checked her watch and realized it was time to take food to Effie. She looked at little Leo and knew instantly there was no way to wrangle him and take food to someone that he had already shown aggression towards. She went out onto the back patio and retrieved a large sitting cushion and took it to her study. There she fluffed it up and sat it on the floor, under her desk.

"This is where you stay for now," she said to Leo, focusing on what she wanted him to do in her mind. To her surprise, he complied, emitting a slight whine as he crawled into the space and curled up on the pillow.

"Okay. Maybe this whole dragon thing won't be so hard after all."

She headed back into the kitchen and quickly heated up a bowl of chicken noodle soup she had purchased in town, lightly toasted some thick slices of counter bread, and placed it on a tray.

Knocking lightly, she entered the room to find Effie sitting upright in her bed, her face toward the large picture window. She smiled, turning to face Torie as she walked into the room.

"Well, that nap must have done you a world of good," said Torie. "You look great. I'm afraid I have to go to the market to get some steaks. But I do have some amazing chicken noodle soup. Are you up for sitting outside? "

"Thank you so much. I feel great. I think all I needed was some good sleep in a comfortable bed, and to feel the sunshine on my face again. But if you don't mind, I think I'll just have my soup here in bed. If that's okay, of course."

Torie sat the tray down next to her.

"Absolutely. The soup is to the left of the tray and some fresh bread to the right for dipping. I placed a glass of water on the nightstand, right in the center. There is nothing else on it to get in the way."

Effie smiled, shaking her head. "You are too good to me. I bet the last thing you wanted was to be taking care of some old fart like me. I'm really feeling better and will be ready to go back home soon enough."

"Honestly, you are no problem at all. I promise you." She squeezed Effie's hand, noting the strength in the woman's grip. "You really are doing much better."

It wasn't just her grip that seemed to have improved, but her entire being. The pallor of her skin didn't seem to be as white, and there was a twinkle to her gray orbs that Torie hadn't noticed before.

"Like I said; a little more rest and I'll be right as rain." She reached confidently for her soup, bringing the spoon to her lips. "This is excellent. Thank you."

"You are welcome. When you've finished, just place the tray over to the side of the bed and I'll be back to collect it."

"Will do," Effie replied, taking another sip. "Oh, Torie, there is something I wanted to ask you. A favor, if I might."

"Of course, anything," Torie said.

"It's about my sister. I haven't seen her in many, many years because my son would never allow her to visit. He wouldn't even let us talk on the phone. I just…I don't mean to take advantage of your kindness, but if I give you a number, can you just call her and let her know that I am alright? And honestly, it would do me a world of good to know she is alright as well. I feel so bad not having spoken to her in so long."

Torie felt bad that she had forgotten all about Effie having a sister. She saw the elder woman's eyebrows knit together in worry and could see that she was close to crying again.

"I am so sorry you and your sister have been kept apart like that. Of course I will call her. It's the very least I could do. Just let me get a pen and paper."

She returned with a spiral-bound note pad and a pen.

"Okay, can you give me her name and number?"

"Her name is Hattie and she's at 555-871-2234. She lives in Salem, Oregon."

Torie wrote everything down and then took out her phone to transfer the information and store it there. It occurred to her as she was doing it that she really didn't have to go looking for a piece of paper; she could have just used her phone from the beginning. She really needed to start relying more on technology, but she loved the feel of paper in her hands.

She once again told Effie she would make the call today and left her to finish her meal. She returned to her study to check in on Leo, who appeared to be napping in his new, comfortable cave. If the old saying was to let sleeping dogs lie, she could not imagine what would be appropriate for sleeping dragons; so, she opted to leave him where he was and instead made her way back to the kitchen.

She flipped open her iPad and started perusing chocolate ideas, hoping for inspiration. A buzzing sound interrupted her thoughts and she looked around distractedly for the source.

There was a sleek, thin video monitor mounted under the cabinet in the corner of the kitchen and on it she could see Jasmin and Fionna standing at the front door. She pressed the talk button, told them to come on in, and then pressed another button to unlock the door.

"I'm in the kitchen," she called.

Seconds later her friends appeared, Fionna marveling at the beautiful furniture and decorations. Torie felt bad as she realized she hadn't involved Fionna in picking out furniture as she had Jasmin..

"Now this—" Fionna said, indicating the surrounding space with a sweep of both arms, "—is how you decorate. Congratulations." She held out a wine bag and offered it to Torie. "A housewarming present."

Torie took the bag graciously. "Thank you, Fionna. But you shouldn't have."

"Nonsense. It's your first home that you own completely, so you need all the gifts as far as I'm concerned. Besides, you're throwing me a birthday party, so I need to give you something. I mean, you are still throwing the party, right?"

Jasmin fixed her with a stare. "We've been over this Fionna."

"What? I'm sorry. Like I said, I absolutely understand if you can't. Your life is crazy right now."

Torie smiled. "Doesn't matter how crazy it gets, the party is still on." She sat the bag on the large island and turned to face them.

"Speaking of crazy, why on earth is Elric bringing a vampire into your house? Especially one from Trinity Cove."

"He said he knows a lot about dragons," replied Torie. "And right now, I need to learn as much as possible about Leo."

"Leo?" said Jasmin, arching an eyebrow. "So you've named it?"

"It isn't a thing, Jasmin. And yes, I have named him."

"Oh, that sounds like a perfect name for a baby dragon," said Fionna. "Where is he? Can I play with him? Oh, did you feed him?"

"I did get him to eat. He seems very fond of raw hamburger. He's napping in the study for now. I've decided to keep him in there when he's not with me; I don't think he was very fond of Effie so I can't have him just exploring the house and wandering into her room."

Jasmin's brow knitted together. "What do you mean not fond? What happened?"

"Well, nothing happened. I went in to check on her and he was with me. He just sort of...lunged at her. And there might have been the tiniest amount of...smoke, coming from him."

"He breathes fire!" said Fionna excitedly.

"He breathes smoke. There was no fire whatsoever."

"He's a dragon," said Jasmin. "Where there's smoke, there will literally be fire at some point. I guess you're right. The more you learn about him the better."

"Especially if he is going to be your familiar," said Fionna.

Jasmin spoke up before Torie could answer.

"I'm not so sure about that. I did a lot of research trying to find out what I could about dragons, well, whatever I could dig up that wasn't Arthurian myth; and I also researched familiars. From what I could find, while familiars are magical creatures, they almost always come in the form of an animal that is somehow familiar to the witch. Hence the name familiars."

"So, cats, dogs, birds…things of that nature?" asked Torie.

"Correct. I could not find any instance of a mythological creature showing up that the witch has no history with."

"So he's here for a different reason then?" said Torie, hiding the slight bit of hurt in her voice.

"We don't know for sure," said Jasmin. "Singing Falls is a town steeped in magic. It could be that he was drawn here for some reason. I just don't know enough about this to hazard a good guess."

"Or maybe he was placed here," said Fionna, taking a seat on one of the bar chairs.

"What do you mean?" asked Torie.

"Well, think about how you found him. You said he was on your porch in a basket, right? Well, what does it mean when human babies are left at the doorstep of hospitals or fire stations?" She glanced briefly at Jasmin, seeing the slight wince she made at the remark. "Oh geez, Jasmin, I didn't mean that in a bad way. I'm sorry; me and my big mouth."

"It's okay," said Jasmin. "You have a point. I left my daughter at the fire station because I knew I couldn't take care of her. I wanted her to have the life I knew I wouldn't be able to provide."

"Yes. So, what if that was the same with Leo? Maybe, whoever had him knew he was beyond their ability to provide for? Kind of like when someone gets a pet alligator or snake and don't realize just how big they get, so they turn them loose or flush them down the sewer."

"You know that's an urban legend, right?" said Torie. "There are no alligators in the sewers."

Both Jasmin and Fionna looked at her, their eyes wide.

"Maybe not where you are from," said Fionna. "But I know a gator-shifter that was raised in a sewer because of that very reason."

Torie was shocked, her mouth dropping open. She headed for the cabinet and took out a bottle of whiskey. This was obviously going to be one of those kinds of conversations.

"Anyway," said Fionna, "all I'm saying is that someone, or something, put him here for a reason."

"If that's the case," said Jasmin, "the next logical question is who and why? Who would have a baby dragon and why would they give it up? And why was it left with Torie?"

"There's another question Implicit in all of this as well," said Torie. "Where are Leo's parents? And is there a mama dragon out there somewhere that will come looking for him."

That was a sobering thought that none of them had an answer for.

Torie poured them all a small whiskey and handed it out. The first sip burned deliciously going down, and all of them coughed slightly and laughed at one another. Just then, another buzz echoed in the kitchen, and Torie went to the monitor to see who was ringing her doorbell.

Elric's face appeared on the screen and he waved at the camera. Beside him stood the tall, lean figure of a man. He stood with his face turned away from the camera as he surveyed the property around him.

The vampire.

Torie took a deep breath and nodded to her friends. Together, they made their way to the front door.

Chapter Ten

Torie swung the big door open and gave Elric an apprehensive look.

"Elric," she said, giving him a nod.

Jasmin and Fionna flanked her, and she could feel the magic buzzing in the air around Jasmin. She glanced at her friend who had not taken her eyes off the slender figure that stood next to Elric. Glancing at Fionna, Torie could see that the squirrel shifter had one hand inside her denim jacket; her eyes were also fixed on the second man on the porch.

"Okay then, let's get the introductions out of the way," said Elric, releasing a deep breath he had been holding. "This is Elion. Elion, this is Jasmin, Fionna, and Torie." He nodded to each of them as he called their names.

"It is very nice to meet you, ladies," said the man. His voice was deep with no affect and very little intonation. Torie strained to pick up any accent he might have, but, to her surprise, there was none. She chided herself briefly. What had she expected? That he would sound like the count from Sesame Street? She searched her memory to see if Arnold had possessed any trace of an accent. He was the only other vampire she had ever met, but to her dismay, she really could not place what his voice had sounded like.

The vampire stepped forward to stand directly next to Elric so the women could have a better view of him. He was tall, even taller than Elric, yet his body was leaner. He wore jeans, a long-sleeved white tee shirt that fit him almost too loosely, and a dark red jacket. His skin did not have the pale coloring that they expected, but rather was a deep olive hue. His eyes were dark brown with flecks of gold that seemed to float around the irises. Jet-black hair framed sharper features and only served to accent his eyes.

All in all, he was a striking figure. But striking or not, he was still a vampire, and none of the women were quite ready to let their guard down.

Elric stepped forward, entering the house.

"It's okay," he said to them. "I can vouch for him. He's one of the good ones."

Torie cleared her throat and stared at Elion. "So, what now? I mean, how does the whole invitation thing work?"

Elion arched an eyebrow and gave Elric a mischievous grin.

"Um, just invite him inside," said Elric.

"Okay. Vampire Elion, I invite you into my home," said Torie, happy that her voice only quivered once during the invitation.

"Vampire Elion?" replied the man, giving her a smile. "So formal. Almost like that show I once saw…True Blood. But you can leave the vampire part off. It's just Elion."

Torie nodded nervously, then stepped aside for him to enter.

He stood there, his eyes tracing the door frame.

"There appears to be some type of ward protecting your threshold," he said. "I'm not sure I can cross through."

"What? Oh that," said Torie. "I forgot about that."

She held out her hand, palm up, and closed her eyes. When she opened them, she nodded to Elion to let him know it was okay to enter.

He gave her a smile and confidently stepped into the entryway of her house. He looked around, nodding at Jasmin and Fionna.

"You have a beautiful home, Torie. Thank you for inviting me in." He frowned slightly, his gaze settling on Jasmin.

"I assure you, there is no need for you to utilize your magic against me. Is that hex power I feel?"

His words caught her off guard, and she narrowed her eyes at him, her power buzzing throughout her body.

"What do you know about hex magic?" she asked.

"I'm sure not as much as you, but it is a power I have encountered before. I am quite familiar with magicks of all types. Each resonates at a different frequency, and hex magic is unique in comparison to all other forms."

Jasmin jutted her chin in his direction. "Then right here and now, vampire, state your intention to do no harm to us."

Elion raised a single eyebrow and slowly nodded. "Very well; I hereby state that I have no interest in harming any of you or creating any kind of violence in this place. My intentions are merely to help."

Jasmin looked at Torie and slowly recalled the magic that had been swimming around her.

"He was speaking the truth. I would have known if he were lying."

"Well, come on in," said Torie, motioning for them to

follow her through the house into the great room. As they sat down, the three women on one side of the room, Elion and Elric on the other, Torie remembered something Elric had once told her. "Elric, I thought you said vampires don't need an invitation to enter someone's house."

"Oh, technically they don't," he replied. "But I just thought it would be nice for you to actually be the one to invite him in. You know, southern courtesy and all that."

Torie shot him a look that let him know they would be talking about that later.

"And hello to you, little shifter," said Elion, nodding to Fionna.

She didn't move but narrowed her eyes in his direction. "Just so you know, I've staked a vamp before, and if you try to hurt Torie or Jasmin, I won't hesitate to dust you as well." She patted the outside of her jacket to drive the point home.

Elion smiled. "A stake made of hardened teak. Good choice."

Fionna started at his words. "How did you know that?"

"I could smell it the minute you opened the door." He crossed his legs, resting his hands in his lap.

Torie looked from him to Elric and back to the vampire. There was something different about this one. He didn't have the fidgety mannerisms of Arnold. He was stoic and assertive at the same time. Something about the way he carried himself told her that he wasn't worried in the least about either Jasmin's magic or Fionna's stake.

"So, I understand that you have a dragon, is that right?"

Torie nodded. "He's sleeping, but I can see if he's awake." She stood up, but Elion motioned for her to stop.

"If possible, I'd like to go to him instead. If that's alright with you, of course."

Torie shrugged. "I guess. He's in my study, just down the hall."

The group stood, following Torie out of the room and headed for the hallway that would lead to her private wing of the house. Elion paused, staring down the opposite hall towards the room where Effie stayed. Giving Elric a glance, he continued on after Torie and Jasmin. Fionna filed in behind the two men, her eyes not leaving Elion's back.

Torie opened the door to her large study slowly, poking her head in to look around. Nothing appeared to have been disturbed. She half expected her books to be torn to shreds and holes to have been gnawed into the walls and furniture. Wasn't that what many of her friends had stated happened when they got a new puppy and had embarked on house training it?

"I made him a little spot under the desk. Just to try and make him comfortable."

"Interesting," said Elion. "Your instincts were to make him a nest I see. Well, they were spot on. Dragons like to feel enclosed. That's why you often find them in hollowed out dens or small caves."

Torie moved to cross the room towards the desk.

"Not yet," said Elion. "Give me just a second."

The vampire stepped forward and glanced around the room, taking the massive space in. Torie wasn't sure, but for just a moment she thought his eyes seemed to sparkle as the gold moats seemed to expand. Then, closing his eyes, he took in several slow, deep breaths, his nostrils quivering slightly with each inhalation.

Finally, he turned back to Torie with a smile and a nod. "Okay, if you would bring him over, that would be great."

Torie moved across the room and ducked down behind the desk.

Leo was crouched there, but he wasn't asleep. His bright, emerald eyes shone in the shadows beneath the desk, and Torie could just make out the wagging of his tail. At least he was happy to see her, so that had to be a plus.

Torie extended her hand and as usual he scampered up her arm to perch on her shoulder. She stood up, cooing slightly to him, and walked over to Jasmin and Fionna, who immediately began to make a fuss over him, forgetting about the vampire in the room with them, and her teak-wood stake.

"Oh there's the cutie little guy," she exclaimed. Torie laughed. You would have thought she had brought out a baby instead of a scaly reptile. Even Jasmin seemed to forget herself as she moved over to scratch and pet Leo's little head.

They felt his body stiffen and realized that the dragon eyes had lit on Elion's lithe form.

The dragon issued a slight hiss and his body seemed to vibrate. In a flash, he leapt from Torie's shoulder, down her arm to land on the floor. Dropping to all fours, he slowly began to advance on Elion, his tiny body seemed incapable of producing the deep, rumble that came from within.

Torie immediately moved to grab him, but Elion waved her off, indicating that it was okay. Reluctantly, she stood, watching as Leo continued his slow advance.

Once the dragon reached Elion, it sniffed at his feet and then walked in a circle around the vampire, sniffing all the while. Once satisfied, it again stopped to face Elion, raising up on its hind legs. The vampire bent down to pick him up, holding him in the palm of one hand.

"Interesting," said Elion.

"What?" asked Elric. "What's so interesting?"

"You mean other than a vampire holding a dragon?" said Jasmin, dryly. "Nope, nothing to see here."

Elion ignored her as he studied the creature in his hand. "What is interesting is his response to me. Elric, did he respond like this to you? Or to you, Fionna?"

Both of them shook their head.

"Maybe it senses danger," said Fionna, her eyes narrowing at the vampire.

"No, I don't think that is the case," Elion said, ignoring the dig that was sent his way. "I believe it is reacting based on Torie's feelings. It is reading her and acting accordingly."

"But I am the one who invited you in. I'm not afraid of you," Torie said.

"But you were. And if you were to search your feelings, I'm betting that you are still a little apprehensive about me."

"Well, considering the only other vampire I've ever known tried to kill me, yes."

At those words, the dragon again vibrated in Elion's hand, issuing a slight hiss. Elion smiled, locking eyes with the dragon, and then deliberately looking away, letting him know that he meant no harm.

"Dragons are incredibly empathic creatures. Some would say that their empathy rises to the level of telepathy in some cases. He is feeding off what you are feeling. That was why it had to check me out for itself, make sure I passed the sniff test, so to speak."

"So, you're saying that this little creature is somehow bonded to Torie?" asked Jasmin.

"Like a familiar? I knew it!" exclaimed Fionna.

"No. Nothing like a familiar. Dragons are not familiars to witches. It is like a human wanting to have a wolf or a lion for a pet. Sure, they can become a pet, but they never lose who they are, and the human is always aware of this, knowing that at any time if they let their guard down, things could end up very…bloody," Elion said. "But a familiar is an extension of a witch; part of her being. But an extension with its own will and personality. Dragons are dragons. They only bond with other dragons."

"Then how do you explain this?" said Jasmin.

Elion thought for a moment.

"Torie, how do you know this is a male? At this age, it is impossible to tell. Also, why did you pick the name Leo?"

"Honestly, I'm not sure. It's just something I felt," she replied. "And now that I think about what you said, something doesn't make sense. Leo had a very hostile reaction to a guest I have staying here in the house. That was someone that I have no negative feelings about at all, so why would he go after her. She couldn't hurt anyone if she tried."

This caught Elion's attention and he looked up from the dragon, locking eyes with Torie.

"And when he had this reaction, what did you do?"

Torie looked around, biting the inside of her lip.

"Torie, what did you do?" asked Jasmin.

"Well, I was worried about Effie and started thinking what if Leo is just aggressive towards humans so I might have just cast a tiny hex to keep him from doing harm."

Jasmin let out a deep sigh but said nothing.

"You subjugated his will," said Elion, returning his attention to the dragon. "Or at least you tried to."

"What no, nothing like that. I would never do that. I just didn't want him hurting anyone until we knew more about him, that's all."

"Well, it wouldn't have worked, even if you tried. Dragons are fairly immune to most forms of magic," Elion said.

"So, then what she did was no big deal, right?" asked Elric.

Elion thought for a moment before answering.

"I said it wouldn't work. I didn't say that it wouldn't have some kind of effect on him. As I said, dragons are incredibly empathetic. Since this one is so very young, it would have taken what you did as an invitation."

"An invitation to what?" said Torie.

"Mind meld. Your hex incantation created a bond that would normally not exist in nature. It would have never worked on a grown dragon, of course, because they would have developed their own personalities. But with a baby? You just imprinted on the creature, and so now it thinks it's part of you."

Torie let out a deep breath staring at Leo. "So how do I break the imprint? Another spell, maybe?"

"Absolutely not," said Elion. "More magic could confuse him even more. Who knows what he might become."

Before anyone could say anything more, they heard a rustling behind them. Effie was standing in the doorway, one hand bracing her against the wall. Her face was upturned slightly, her head tilted in Torie's direction.

"Torie, is that you? I heard strange voices and became frightened."

Leo saw the old woman at the same time as everyone else. The little dragon narrowed its green eyes and leapt to the ground. Before anyone could stop him, he reared back and blew a large, orange fireball in her direction.

Chapter Eleven

Elric moved first, throwing himself at Effie with all the
speed he could muster. To Elion, he might as well have been
standing still, however.

The vampire's form blurred as he raced to place himself
between the blind woman and the fireball. The flames
struck his back, breaking into a shower of sparks that fell
harmlessly to the ground. Elion's jacket and shirt were
incinerated upon contact, and his skin began to bubble,
reminding Torie of a post of slowly simmering spaghetti
sauce.

In an instant it was over. Torie rushed forward to scoop
up Leo.

"No, Leo! Bad dra...kitty. You don't do that," she
peeked around Elion at Effie. The older woman seemed
fine, her face contorted in confusion.

"Torie, what's going on. Was that your cat acting up
again? And who are these people? Why is it so hot in here?"
She was within inches of Elion's form, but was unaware he
was there. Silently, the vampire backed away from her as

she slowly inched into the room, feeling the space before her with one hand.

"Oh, it's just me, Fionna." She rushed forward and took Effie's hand. "Jasmin and I just stopped by to help Torie plan a party."

"Oh, Fionna, hello dear. But I thought I heard a man's voice?"

"Oh, that's me, ma'am," said Elric, stepping forward to stand next to Fionna. "I'm just here helping with the furniture moving and installation."

"Oh, a party! I do love a good party. I hope I get an invite."

"Oh, you are going to be the guest of honor," said Fionna. "But what say we get you back to your bed? Or what if I take you out onto the patio for some fresh air? It's a beautiful evening."

Effie's gray eyes grew large with excitement. "Oh yes, I would like that. If it's not too much of a problem for you."

"Not at all," Fionna said, turning the woman around and leading her down the hall. She cast a look over her shoulder at Torie and shrugged. "I won't keep her outside too long."

Once they were gone from sight, Jasmin was the first to speak up.

"What the hell just happened? Did that little critter just try to flash-fry that old woman?"

"I don't understand where that came from," said Torie. "You see, I am not the least bit apprehensive towards Effie, and he reacts like this. I don't get it."

"Interesting indeed," said Elion, his voice low as he looked down the corridor where Fionna and Effie had disappeared.

"Oh my god, your skin," said Jasmin as she moved over to stand beside Elion.

Torie and Elric turned their attention back to Elion's charred and blistering flesh. Torie put a hand to her mouth in shock. The burns had deepened but at least it no longer resembled a rolling boil. She placed Leo down so she could get a better look at the vampire.

"Oh, it's nothing. I can already feel it healing," said Elion.

He was right. Even as they watched, patches of charred skin were slowly beginning to return to the normal olive tone, matching the rest of his body. The blisters bubbled, working their way through the healing process as well.

"That's incredible," said Jasmin. "Does it hurt?"

"Yes, but not as much as you might think."

"So, you're immune to dragon fire," said Jasmin.

"To baby dragon fire," corrected Elion. "I don't think I'd have the same outcome with a fully grown one."

"But this tells us that this dragon is dangerous," said Elric. "What do we do with it?"

Torie frowned, not liking the implication in Elric's words. "We don't do anything with it except find out why he's here, and where he belongs."

"I wasn't implying anything else," said Elric. "But that was a little extreme. I mean, he literally breathed fire."

"That's what dragons do," said Elion. "Among other things."

"Like what?" asked Torie. "What else do you know about them?"

"They are poisonous as well," replied the vampire. "The same sacs in their throats that produce fire are also capable of creating a toxin. Also, the spikes in their tails are detachable; a quick whip of their tale can send them flying like razor sharp, unbreakable pieces of shrapnel."

The room was silent as all eyes fell on Leo. The dragon had returned to his perch on Torie's shoulder and was contentedly playing with a strand of her hair.

"Well, other than the fire, he hasn't shown any proclivities for all that," said Torie, reaching up to absentmindedly pet him.

"Yet," said Jasmin.

Torie ignored her, turning her attention back to Elion. "What about his parents? How would a dragon have appeared on my doorstep like this?"

"I've been thinking about that, and I don't really have a good answer. Dragons this age are almost always under the protection of their mother. As you can imagine, they are incredibly protective creatures; so I can't imagine one handing their child over to someone."

"So, the mother is probably dead," said Elric.

Elion shrugged. "I can't see any other way that a baby would come to be here in Singing Falls. And as far as that goes, dragons are not native to North Carolina. Truthfully, with the possible exception of the northern California coast, and parts of Alaska, they aren't native to the Americas at all. They are almost exclusively found in Africa and Asia. The ones that are here in the States are transplants, brought here by traders from the aforementioned countries and stranded; I, myself, have only ever seen one. She was so old that she barely moved. Her body had become part of the rock around her. The tribes that knew of her existence worshiped her as a living spirit. But those people died off long ago, and to my knowledge, no one else knew of her existence."

Torie frowned. "How long ago are we talking?"

Elion thought for a moment. "Maybe, four or five hundred years ago. And as I said, she was ancient at that time."

"Wait, how old does that make you?" asked Jasmin.

Elion didn't immediately answer. "Let's just say that I left my homeland during the great wars because I was tired of the bloodshed. I made my way here long before your country was officially discovered."

"What wars are we talking about? World wars...or what?" said Jasmin.

"The Crusades."

Torie saw Jasmin's jaw drop. After some quick math, so did hers.

"And I was considered very old at that point. Even I am not entirely sure how old I am. And dragons, some that I have heard of at least, are far older than me. They predate all supernatural creatures by millennia."

"But they aren't magical, right?" asked Jasmin.

"Depends on what you mean by magical. Do they cast spells or manipulate magic the way you do? No. But they are part of the ecosystem that allows magic to exist. You might say they are the sun-source of all mystical powers. The fact that your magic exists in this world is due to their presence."

"So that's why they are pretty much immune to magic then," said Torie. "But why would Leo have been susceptible to my spells then?"

Elion shook his head. "I have no idea. Unless it has to do with his age, as I said."

"So, all of that still does not tell us how Leo got here," said Torie, looking at the little dragon, "or why he was so aggressive towards a human."

"I have a feeling there are a lot of questions that remain

to be answered here," said Elion. "Questions that you probably haven't thought to ask yet."

Something in his tone and the wording he used scratched at the back of Torie's mind; something she had forgotten but was on the verge of remembering.

"Oh well, thank you for the info," said Elric. "I guess we better head back to Trinity Cove so you can get settled in before sunrise, huh?"

Elion glanced at the werewolf, but then turned to Torie.

"Torie, if you would be okay with it, I would like to stay. Just for a bit. I would like to observe your little dragon a little more, if that would be alright."

Torie and Jasmin exchanged nervous looks. Thankfully, Fionna was still outside, because they could only imagine the response she would have given.

"I promise I won't be any trouble," Elion said. "You will hardly even know I'm here. Plus, I don't eat anything, so you don't have to worry about that."

"Well, technically, that isn't true," said Elric.

His demeanor had changed completely. Gone was the buddy-buddy attitude he had displayed with Elion earlier. He had quickly morphed into the creature that protected his mate with his life.

Elion waved his hand dismissively in the air. "Elric, you know that I don't feed very often, and when I do it's only on animals. Usually the old and dying ones that would not have lasted much longer anyway."

"Somehow that doesn't give me a lot of confidence, so the answer is no," Jasmin said.

"Um, I have to agree," said Elric. "We really should be heading back."

"Is that what you want, Torie?" asked Elion, not bothering to look at her friends.

She looked at him hard, weighing her options. On one hand, she wanted to learn all she could about Leo in order to help him. On the other hand, there was the thought of death by vampire, and she really wasn't very keen on that. But, searching her feelings, something told her she could trust Elion. She knew her answer as soon as he asked the question.

"He can stay. But just until we figure out what to do with Leo."

Jasmin clicked her tongue, shaking her head. Elric said nothing, but Torie could see his eyes darken as he looked around the room.

"But I don't know where you'll sleep or what you'll need. I don't have a coffin or a room that is blacked out from the light."

"I don't sleep in a coffin, Torie. I also don't need a room that is blacked out. A normal guest room is fine."

"Wait, so you aren't afraid of the sun?" asked Jasmin.

Elion shook his head. "Of course not. You won't find me lying outside soaking up the rays, but at my age, sunlight is uncomfortable to be exposed to; but it won't kill me."

Jasmin gave Torie a look that let her know they were probably both having the same thought.

If sunlight can't kill him, what can?

"Well, then I guess that settles it?" said Jasmin as she gathered her purse and headed for the door. "I'll be back in just a bit with my things."

"What things? Why are you coming back?" asked Fionna as she entered the room.

"Torie has decided to let Elion stay here for a bit, so I'm going home to pack a bag. I'll be sleeping here as well." She gave the vampire a long stare before continuing for the door.

"Honestly, Jasmin, you live right beside me; you're two minutes away. I don't think—" She was interrupted by Fionna taking her phone out and pacing the room as she made a call. "And what are you doing, Fionna?"

"I'm calling Glen and having her bring me my overnight bag and my big stake." She also gave Elion a stare. "Just in case."

Torie raised both hands in the air before letting them drop in exasperation. She gave Elric a glance and could see the werewolf smiling, the storm in his eyes now a bemused twinkle.

"And you?" she asked him.

"Oh, it's a slumber party now. This will be fun," he replied.

His phone chirped and he fished it out, glancing at the screen.

"Max just texted. He has the preliminary autopsy report on the mayor. He's coming by in the morning with some news."

In all honesty, Torie had nearly forgotten about the mayor, what with everything going on.

"Well, I guess we can figure out where everybody can sleep," said Torie.

Jasmin looked around, waving a hand at her surroundings. "You've got about seven thousand square feet here, Torie. I think we can all find a place. Besides, isn't this what you envisioned when you built this place? Room for all who needed a place to stay?" She smiled, her voice trailing off as she dug her keys out of her purse and headed for the door before stopping to turn back around to look at Elion. "What about the wards? Can they go back up?"

Elion looked away, staring out the office window into the darkness of the woods.

"If it makes you feel safer, of course. But once they are up, I will not be able to leave the premises at all, even if I wanted to."

"So, dragon fire and sunlight don't hurt you, but you can't pass through magical wards?" said Torie. "Good to know. Well, since we are all here, I'll go open a couple bottles of wine and see if I can throw together some snacks. I have a feeling it's going to be a long night."

Chapter Twelve

She had been right of course. Everyone was too on edge to sleep, and when the first rays of morning light broke through the highest of the windows along the back of the house, Torie felt like her eyelids weighed ten pounds each.

"Whew, I am out of practice," said Jasmin as they sat in the kitchen.

Torie had placed a large pot of water on to boil and had filled the coffee maker. "Practice with what?"

"Keeping my ass up all night. I can't remember the last time I pulled an all-nighter for anything."

"I haven't done it since Shawn was a baby. He had colic and would sometimes cry for hours at a time at night. The only thing that I found would help was to strap him into a car seat and place that on top of the dryer. So I'd sit there for half the night with him like that. Didn't think he would ever grow out of that."

The mention of her son made her both sad and elated. Sad because she missed him but elated because she knew that he was sure to come for a visit soon. He had not yet seen the new house and she was excited to show him his room and let him put his finishing touch on it. It was the only room that she had told her guests was off limits to them.

Otherwise, she had given them free rein and let them pick whichever room they wanted. Everyone had stowed their things, only to regroup in the great room. Light banter had turned to silence around four in the morning, and everyone spent the next couple of hours dozing and waking with a start.

Everyone except Elion.

Torie had watched the vampire as he sat in a wing-back chair next to the huge fireplace, one leg casually draped over the other. He hadn't spoken throughout the night, his keen eyes seemed to be focused on something in the distance. Each time Torie would nod off and wake with a start, he would still be in the exact same position, his eyes locked on either her or Leo, who slept curled in a ball on a pillow next to where she sat with Elric on the couch.

Elric had also not slept, remaining motionless, his attention focused solely on Torie. Every time she opened her eyes, she felt his hand on hers giving her a reassuring squeeze.

"Is it just me or do supernaturals not sleep?" asked Torie. "I don't think Elric or Elion closed their eyes once all night. It was freaky."

"And neither did Fionna," said Jasmin. "That girl sat there holding that stake in a death grip, staring at Elion the whole night." She chuckled slightly at the image.

"What time do you think Max will be here?" asked Torie.

"Probably any minute now. Especially as soon as you

throw some bacon on that griddle, he'll smell it and come running."

Torie laughed. "I guess that's a hint huh?"

She opened the fridge and took out an enormous package of applewood smoked bacon. Jasmin had been kind enough to raid her pantry and refrigerator and bring over enough supplies to feed a small army. Elion might not eat food, but Elric and Max could put away more food at one sitting than a family of four in a week. And for someone so petite, Fionna was nearly a match for them.

Jasmin helped to set out dishes and cutlery when something small brushed against her leg unexpectedly. She let out a small scream and nearly dropped the coffee cups she was holding. Looking down, she saw Leo glancing up at her as he continued to rub his body across the back of her legs.

"Torie, I think your dragon thinks he's a cat."

Torie rushed around the island to pick him up, cooing at him as if he were an infant.

"Oh, he's probably hungry. He hasn't eaten since yesterday, and I have no idea how often to feed a dragon."

"That depends on how big you want them to grow." It was Elion. He was leaning against the wall behind them, staring at Leo. "They are much like the reptiles that evolved from them. Meaning, they can grow to the size of their surroundings and to match the supply of food around them."

"If that's true," said Jasmin, "then with the size of this house, you're in trouble, Torie. And where did you come from, Elion? You can't just go around popping up out of nowhere like that. Maybe someone should put a bell on you."

Her remark at least got a smile out of the vampire. "My kind have very light footsteps."

"So we see," said Torie. She looked at the coffee and then at Elion. "I'm making breakfast, which I know you don't eat, but what about coffee? Can you drink that?"

Elion frowned. "Honestly, I don't know. I've never tried it. I don't eat solids because I have no way of digesting them. The…fluids I ingest travel directly to my circulatory system, providing what little nutrients my body requires to continue functioning. I suppose I can try coffee. I have always enjoyed the smell but have never actually attempted to drink it."

"Well, then I am happy to be your first," said Torie.

"Your first what?" asked Elric, walking lazily into the room.

"Provider of coffee. Nothing more," replied Torie.

"So, Elion, how often do you need to feed?" asked Jasmin.

"Once or twice a month at this point."

"That's not very often. What happens if you don't feed?" Jasmin pressed.

"Well, if I stop drinking, eventually I will stop moving. My body will not atrophy beyond this point, but I will grow cold and motionless. My mind may continue, or it may not. I have heard stories of vampires who have reached a certain age and become bored with life—or non-life in our case— and simply retired to a remote location and became still. So still that the forest grew over them, claiming their bodies and pulling them deep into the root systems of trees and plants. Are those vampires still alive on the inside? I don't know. I don't even know if those stories are true."

"Well, that sounds macabre," said Torie, "and hardly breakfast conversation." She turned her attention to the beeping coffee pot and removed the carafe of dark brew.

Pouring a cup, she placed it in front of the vampire as all eyes turned to him.

Jasmin took out her phone and aimed it at him as he picked up the cup, eyeing it cautiously.

"What? I'm recording this moment for prosperity. How often will we have an ancient vampire drinking his first cup of coffee in your house?" she said.

Slowly, Elion raised the cup to his lips and took a small sip. He looked up, giving a smile to Jasmin's camera.

"It's good," he proclaimed. He took a second, longer drink. "Very good." He threw back his head and downed the entire cup of steaming brew in a single gulp, much to everyone's surprise. "May I have another?"

"Um, sure," said Torie. "But just so you know, most people drink it slowly, in sips. Not that it matters here, but if you were ever to have some out in public, that would definitely draw attention to you."

After sitting another cup in front of him, and pouring more for her guests, Torie set about preparing bacon and eggs while Elric cut up fresh fruit and laid it out on a platter.

"Has anyone seen Fionna?" Torie asked.

"She took Effie out for a walk earlier. Those two seem to have really hit it off," said Jasmin.

The mention of Effie's name caught Elion's attention. "Torie, may I spend some time with your houseguest? I'd like to talk to her."

She had been in the midst of fluffing the giant skillet of scrambled eggs and stopped to look at him.

"No. I don't think that is wise. She's been through a lot and we can't figure out what to do with her. I can't see any reason that you might have to speak with her."

"What interest do you have in her?" asked Jasmin.

Elion waved dismissively before taking another draw of coffee. "It's nothing. I find older humans intriguing is all."

"That reminds me," said Torie. "She told me she has a sister that her son would never let her speak with. She wants me to check in with her and gave me her number out west. I had planned on calling her today once we speak with Max. I should have done it last night. But there was so much going on."

"A sister," said Jasmin. "So she does have family. Looks like you might not have to host a guest too much longer, Torie."

"Funny how Max's contacts came up empty on finding her family though," said Elric. "Between that and the fact that she doesn't show up in any records in the mayor's background, it almost feels like someone kept her hidden all this time."

"Someone as in the mayor," said Torie. She placed the eggs on a platter and then the bacon. She piled some uncooked pieces onto a paper plate for Leo and placed it on the floor, giving him a little mental nudge letting him know it was okay to eat.

"What did you just do?" asked Elion. He stood up from the table and came to crouch by the dragon as it eagerly feasted on the raw meat.

"What do you mean?" asked Torie.

"Just now. When you fed him. I felt something from you...a push almost."

"Oh that. I found that if I form a mental image of what I want him to do, he will sometimes do it. It's starting to become a reflex I think."

Elion looked from the dragon to her and then back to the dragon.

"Indeed," he said, standing to return to his coffee.

Torie looked at Jasmin, who nodded her head in the direction of the great room and casually walked out of the kitchen. Torie wiped her hands on the dishtowel and followed her. Once outside the kitchen, Jasmin leaned in, whispering to her.

"I don't trust that vampire. I've known vampires before and this one is not like any I've ever come across. How was he able to pick up on you sending an almost unconscious message to a dragon like that? Even I didn't feel anything from you."

"Maybe not all vampires are alike. Maybe they possess different powers; or maybe they just have senses that develop over time that you don't know anything about. How should I know?"

"But that's just it; what do we know about him? I mean, sure, he has given us some good information about Leo, but why would he want to stay? Why the interest in old miss Effie? I saw the way he looked at her last night as well. It's more than just liking to chat with old people as he claims. I'm not buying it. Plus, Fionna is really on edge around him, and she has great instincts."

"And so do I," said Torie. "I just don't get the feeling that he is a danger."

Jasmin placed her hands on her hips and stared at her friend.

"Not a danger? He's impervious to dragon fire, and sunlight, and he's old as dirt. That means he's powerful. We have no idea what he's capable of. He may not be human but I'm betting he still falls under human nature—meaning he will ask for something at some point." They were headed back into the kitchen where Torie was pleased to see there was some light banter going on between Elric and Elion.

Elion turned to them with a smile. "You forgot one

other thing. I have amazing hearing." He then drained his coffee cup and sat it in the sink before heading out of the kitchen.

As he walked out, Max walked in, giving the vampire a long stare.

"You really shouldn't just leave your door unlocked like that," he said to Torie.

"Thanks, Max. But this house has three shifters, two witches and a vampire kicking around. I feel sorry for anyone who picked now to break in."

"And was that...Elion?" he said to Elric.

The other wolf nodded, and Max gave a low whistle. "Definitely need to keep an eye on him."

Jasmin's ears perked up. "Why would you say that?"

"Because he's a vampire. Why else?"

Torie let out a deep breath. "Max, what were you able to find out about the mayor's death?"

The sheriff had a manilla folder in his hands which he opened, laying the paper contents onto the island.

"Well, the medical examiner found evidence of a massive stroke. His brain was filled with blood. He died of a sudden hemorrhage. Probably didn't feel anything."

"So he died of natural causes," said Jasmin.

"That's what it looked like, until the M.E. found this." He shuffled through the papers until he came to photos of the dead mayor's body. One of the photos was an extreme close-up of an area on the top of the mayor's hand that focused in on a small black dot.

"What is it?" asked Torie.

"The M.E. said it was a tiny puncture. Not much bigger than the head of a pin. Closer examination of it showed that it was an injection site. Someone shot him up with something that caused his bleed."

Torie took a deep breath. "So, it looks like Singing Falls has a murderer running loose. Great. How the heck am I supposed to plan a party and make chocolates while unpacking and taking care of our murder victim's aging mother, babysit a dragon and an ancient vampire, all while a murderer is on the loose?"

"Well, it gets better," said Max, reaching into his jacket pocket. He withdrew an older model cellphone and opened it. He keyed in a sequence of numbers to unlock it. "We found this while we were searching his house. It was hidden in the back drawer of a file cabinet in his home office. This was one of the saved voice files."

He pressed another key a couple of times, skipping through voice memo recordings until he got to the one he wanted them to hear.

"I don't know what else to do. I'm out of options." The voice was male and sounded quite scared.

"Maybe you should just leave town. She's going to get to you sooner or later," came a second voice. This one female and just as scared sounding.

"I can't just leave her like that. I know what I have to do."

"You don't know what you're in for. Those witches are not to be toyed with," replied the female.

"You're right of course. Torie Bliss may well be the last face I see. If something happens to me, you know what to do." The line went dead after that, and no one in the room spoke.

"Torie Bliss," said Max, "I need you to come with me to the station to answer some questions. If you have a lawyer, it might be a good time to give them a call."

Chapter Thirteen

"What? You're arresting her?" demanded Jasmin in dismay.

"No, of course not. But from a procedural standpoint, I need to take her downtown for questioning."

"Like hell you do," said Jasmin. Her eyes flared and blue orbs of magic encircled her hands.

"Don't touch her, Max," said Elric. The wolf's eyes glowed yellow and his voice deepened. Torie knew that look and knew that he was on the brink of shifting and squaring off against his old alpha.

"Okay, everybody just calm down," she said. "Max, you know I had nothing to do with killing the mayor. I never even met the man."

"Why is he talking to someone about you trying to kill him then?" Max asked.

"He didn't say she was trying to kill him, he mentioned something about her being the last face he'd ever see. Big difference. Plus, that wasn't a voicemail; it was a recording of a conversation. Maybe that means he was speaking with someone that he didn't trust. Maybe he wanted dirt on whoever that was."

"Max, you were at the scene of his death just like we were. You yourself said there was no other scent in the vehicle with him, right?" said Torie.

Max nodded. "But he wasn't killed at the crime scene. He was most likely injected somewhere else and then died in the car."

Torie didn't like the way this was going. She was pretty sure Max knew she had nothing to do with this, but what about other law enforcement officials? The murder of a mayor had to attract eyes higher up than his.

"This has federal implications," said Max, confirming Torie's suspicions. "The cleaner we make our paperwork dealing with the investigation, the better in the long run."

The words federal stuck in Torie's mind. What if they focused in on her because of her previous dealings with them because of her husband? He had taken the fall for a massive Ponzi scheme that was orchestrated by his lover, a fae woman with whom he had had a child. While Torie had been completely cleared of any involvement, she wasn't so sure that they wouldn't use this as an opportunity to open another file on her. That kind of scrutiny was the last thing she needed right now.

"Max, have you identified the other person on the message?" asked Jasmin.

"No, not yet. We have no clue who she is."

"Well, that sounds like a good place to start. Let us help you. What happened to the mayor is a tragedy; but right now, you've made this personal. Just give us a couple of days to work on this, and if we don't get you any information, I'll walk Torie down to you myself," Jasmin said, looking over at her friend. "But I promise you it won't come to that."

"Max, there has to be a way you can slow this down, just for a couple of days," said Elric. "You owe us that."

Torie stepped between them, once again pleading for calmer heads to prevail. "Look, it's no big deal. I have nothing to hide. If Max needs me to come down to the station, then I will. I don't have a lawyer, however, so I'll need help with that."

Max looked from Torie to her friends and took a deep breath.

"Once your name is tied in any way to this, things will get messy for you. The feds are going to want someone to pin this on and, honestly, in a small, backwater community like this, they might not care who. I'll keep you out of this for forty-eight hours. Bring me something I can use."

"You can use me," said Elion, walking slowly back into the room.

Max flinched and narrowed his eyes at the vampire.

"I could not help but overhear what was happening. I think I can be of some help to you. Have your labs been able to identify the toxin that was used on your mayor?"

"No. So far it doesn't match up with any known poisons in our database."

"Ah, well in that case, maybe I can help you identify it."

"How would you do that?" asked Torie.

"I need to taste a sample of the victim's blood," Elion replied in an almost nonchalant way. "I will be able to taste everything that was in his system at the time of his death, right down to where the beans in the coffee he drank for breakfast were grown."

"That sounds gross," said Jasmin.

"Trust me, it is not something I am looking forward to. Sampling a dead man's blood is not a pleasant thing. It would be like you drinking milk that has clotted, soured and then been left out so long it has grown fungus. Times ten. But I will be able to identify the elements that make up the poison. At least that will be a start for you."

Jasmin nodded. "And in the meantime, we can start tracking down this mystery woman on the phone."

"Where would we even start?" asked Torie.

"That's easy. His mother is staying here. Granted, she was pretty much held prisoner by him, but maybe she would have a clue about her son's comings and goings. Plus, I'm pretty sure we can nudge her memory a little if need be," said Jasmin.

Torie frowned. "That seems like it would be an invasion of privacy."

"It will be a last resort, I promise. Plus, it might help her in the long run too."

"Alright, so we have a plan," said Max. "Or at least the bare bones of one. Elion, how do you want to do this? It's daylight out there. I know the sun won't kill you, but do you really want to risk a severe burn right now?"

"What if you bring the car into the garage?" said Torie. "That way he can get into it without direct exposure."

Max was nodding. "That could work. Then, at the medical office, we can pull into the bay there, so again you're not in direct light. What do you think?"

"I think that sounds like an excellent idea," the vampire said. "Plus, it will give the two of us time to catch up." He patted Max on the back and headed for the back of the house where the mudroom led to the garage.

"Oh, Max, can you send that message from the mayor's phone to my phone?" asked Torie.

Max frowned before answering. "I'm not so sure that's a good idea. But here—" He sat the phone down on the coffee table. "Keep it. I'll just need it back in a couple of days."

Torie thanked the sheriff as he nodded to them and then followed Elion down the hall.

Once there was just the two of them in the room, Torie turned to Jasmin.

"Fionna should be back with Effie anytime, but before we speak with her, I want to call her sister. I'd like to give Effie some good news after everything she has been through," Torie said.

"That's fine. You do that. I'm going to start putting dishes into the washer for you and cleaning up the kitchen."

Torie started to protest but knew that it would fall on deaf ears. Instead, she gathered Leo onto her shoulder and went back into the office where she had left her notebook with Effie's sister's contact information.

She double checked that the number she put into her cell was the same and then settled back onto the small loveseat that occupied a corner of the room.

The phone rang a few times before a pensive voice answered.

"Hello, Effie?" said a woman's voice.

Torie was taken aback but managed to speak up after clearing her throat.

"No, my name is Torie Bliss, I am a friend of your sister's. Is this Hattie?"

"Yes, yes it is," said the woman, the pace of her speaking was picking up in excitement.

"It is very nice to speak with you, ma'am. I wanted to let you know that your sister is here with me at my home and, well, she wanted me to reach out to you and let you know she is safe. She also wants to inquire about how you are doing."

"Oh, thank goodness she is alright! I have been so very worried. May I speak with her? Please?"

"Well, of course you can. She is out on a walk with a friend of mine, but they should be back any minute now. And can I ask…how did you know that I was calling about your sister?"

"She is the only person that has this number. We don't have any other family so my phone only rings when it is her. And it hasn't rang in so very long. Why, I was starting to fear that my no-good nephew had done something awful to her."

Torie didn't say anything, letting that hang in the air. She wasn't sure how to respond, but as luck would have it, she was rescued by the sound of Fionna and Effie returning.

"Hattie, one moment, I think your sister just stepped back in." She placed Leo in his makeshift cave and left the study, closing the door behind her.

She could hear Fionna laughing lightly at something Effie said and was able to catch them as they headed down the hall toward the guest room.

"Effie," she called after them, holding her phone in the air, "I have your sister on the line. She would like to speak to you."

Effie spun in place to face Torie. She held out her hand, her face overcome with excitement.

"Hattie? Is that really you?" she asked.

Torie could not make out what was being said on the other line, but she could see the tears running down the older woman's face. She was nodding along to whatever Hattie was saying to her, the occasional, "yes" and "of course" slipping out.

"Oh, Hattie, you just don't know how terrible it's been. You know poor Terry has died in a terrible accident. This nice woman has been kind enough to open her home to me until I can go back to my house. Yes...oh I know...yes. Okay, I can ask but I've already been such a bother."

She took the phone from her ear and turned in Torie's direction.

"Torie, you have been so good to me and I hate to ask one more favor, but would it be possible for my sister to come visit me here? She said she can help me get back on my feet and will stay with me at my house as long as she is needed."

Torie looked at Fionna who just shrugged, and then back to Effie.

"Of course she can. I would be honored to meet her," Torie replied.

The tears flowed down Effie's face. "I don't know how to thank you for this." She placed the phone back to her ear. "You hear that, Hattie? You can come visit." She nodded and exchanged a few more pleasantries with her sister before handing the phone back to Torie. "Can you give her your address? I'm going to go lie down again. I fear all this excitement has been a bit much for me."

Torie took the phone as Effie gently grasped Fionna's elbow and was led back to her room. A couple of minutes later, Torie ended the call after providing the requested information to Hattie and walked back into the kitchen.

"What was all that about?" asked Jasmin.

"You know Effie's sister I mentioned? Well, that was her. She's coming to visit Effie and has offered to stay with her at her own house as long as needed to get Effie back on her feet.

"You mean the sister that doesn't exist according to a police database?"

Torie waved her off. "Please, you know as well as I do

that the police in this town are just this side of useless. I mean, they just pegged me as a person of interest in the murder of a man I'd never heard of until we found his dead body."

Jasmin laughed. "Well, we really need to get started on making sure he knows to not even pull your name into this. So, that means, it's time to talk to your houseguest back there and see what she knows."

"Do we have to do it right now? She's exhausted from her walk and the excitement of being reunited with her sister."

"Oh, I don't know, Torie. Do you want to stay off Max's murder radar or would you rather wait until later?"

Torie tsked at her friend. "You don't have to be sarcastic, you know."

"I just don't want you getting caught up in something you have no business being a part of. I do have another idea though."

"What's that?"

"Why don't you and I head over to the mayor's house and look around? I want to try and get a better feeling for the magic that was used on his mother. I still can't figure out how a human could conjure up something like that, and why he would use it to bind his aging mother to a bed. I have a feeling that his death is tied to that."

"That sounds like an excellent plan. But can we stop at the specialty market on the way back? I have an idea for a special candy I want to create for the festival contest. Plus, I need to place the order for flowers for Fionna's party."

Jasmin shook her head, smiling in admiration. "I don't know where you're finding this energy, but so be it. What about your dragon? Do you trust him here alone?"

Torie hadn't thought about that but knew there was no way to take him with her.

"I'll leave him in the study. Fionna can watch Effie and keep an eye on Leo. What's the worst that could happen?"

Jasmin arched a single eyebrow. "Don't ever say something like that. Especially not where Fionna is concerned."

They finished cleaning the kitchen, and Torie went in to check on Fionna and Effie. Effie was resting quietly on her bed while Fionna was curled in the reading chair next to the window. Rather than wake her, Torie scribbled a note and left it on the table next to the napping shifter. Then she checked in on Leo and found him curled in a ball in his little hideaway. She gave him a scratch on the head and left the office, pulling the door shut behind her.

Chapter Fourteen

The drive to the mayor's house was uneventful, and they passed the time listening to one of Jasmin's favorite 80s stations. While it wasn't Torie's favorite, they both agreed it stood head and shoulders above the awful pop music that lately seemed to dominate the airwaves.

Easing into the long driveway that led to the home, they were greeted with yellow police tape cordoning off the front porch. Torie had forgotten it was an active crime scene, and entering it made her all the more nervous.

"What if I leave a hair or the feds come in and find my fingerprints? Won't that make me look like more of a suspect?"

"No, because we were already in the house, they will have established trace evidence from both of us and discounted it."

"Still, I wish we had come at night."

"It's not like there is any surveillance here, so no one is going to see us. And if you're worried about leaving hair or DNA, I'm pretty sure that would still happen even if we were in the dark. Probably more likely then, because I can't see anything at night anymore without my glasses."

They walked up to the house and slipped under the police tape before reaching the front door. There was another band of tape, this time red, that spanned the width of the door. Torie knew there was no turning back now; once they broke the tape by opening the door, they would officially be breaking the law.

Jasmin waved her hand, her magic tearing through the tape and forcing the locked door open. Inside, the house was deathly still and quiet. It was amazing how lonely a house could feel once its human occupants left it to its own devices.

Torie reached out with her magic, sending a thread of her hex power snaking through the house to make sure they were truly alone. Satisfied there was no one else there with them, she nodded to Jasmin and together they made their way deeper inside. The house was a center hall colonial, so there were open spaces to the left and right of the staircase.

"You take the right side, I'll take the left," said Jasmin. "Look for his office or any space that might look like somewhere to hide something."

Torie nodded and moved off to her right, into the dining area. There was a small rectangular table in the middle of the room, flanked by two chairs on either side. A long sideboard took up one wall and arranged on top were tiny sculptures and decorative canisters. Looking through them she realized they were all empty and purely for decoration. The cabinet space beneath the sideboard contained stacks of china and a box containing silverware.

She moved on into the kitchen and began looking through the drawers and cabinets, not finding anything that didn't belong in a kitchen. Just as she was about to close the last cabinet, she felt something.

It was like a shadow that she didn't see, but rather felt, as it glided swiftly by, passing through the room. It was so abrupt that had she been holding a cup it would have dropped to the tile floor and shattered. She bolted from the kitchen, back to the stairway where an equally startled Jasmin was standing, looking around in concern.

"I thought you said this place was empty," said Jasmin.

"I thought it was. I don't remember sensing any presence, human or otherwise."

Jasmin looked up the stairway. "I think it went up there."

Torie nodded, letting out a deep breath. She could feel the tiny hairs on the back of her neck stand up as they slowly ascended. Once at the top of the landing, each of the witches probed the space, trying to home in on the source of the disturbance they felt.

"I don't feel anything," said Torie. "Just like before. Could we have imagined it?"

"Both of us? Imaging the same thing at the same time? Doubtful. No, whatever it is, it's up here."

"Okay, but we are not separating to look for it," said Torie. "That's how people that are too stupid to live end up dying."

Jasmin nodded in agreement as they decided where to go. Jasmin pointed to the room at the end of the hall from the landing. That was where they had found the mother mystically bound to her bed, so it was the most obvious choice.

The door to the room was closed, secured with another piece of police tape. This time, Jasmin kept the blue streak of magic at the ready after using it to push open the door.

The room beyond was exactly as they remembered it; the only difference being the closet door had been flung open and obviously searched.

Torie extended a hand and wrapped the bed in magic.

"No trace of anything. Whatever he was using to bind her is no longer here."

Jasmin dropped her magic, placing her hands on her hips. "It just makes no sense. Where would he get such power, and why would he use it on his mother? The woman is old and blind. All he had to do was lock the door and she couldn't go anywhere. This just feels like overkill."

"Come on, there are two more bedrooms on this floor. Let's check them."

Together, they moved down the hall, coming to a second door. This had obviously been a guest room as it was made up impeccably. Plenty of plush, decorative pillows were piled on top of the bedding and the nightstand next to it contained an empty glass water pitcher and two glasses. There was a rocking chair in one corner with freshly folded towels placed on the seat. Again, neither of the witches felt anything out of place.

That left one last room at the far end of the second floor.

Opening the door, they walked into the master bedroom and both were met with a stench that made them gag. Covering their nose with their elbows, they looked at each other and summoned a protective shield that only partially obstructed the putrid smell.

"What in the world is that?" asked Torie.

"Something old and dead." Jasmin's eyes narrowed as she peered into the room.

The windows were covered with heavy drapes that blocked out any light, making the room appear hazy and gray. The space was large, with an unmade bed against one wall facing the window. The two nightstands were both overflowing with papers, charging cables, paperclips and electronic vaping cartridges. There were dirty clothes and socks on the floor strewn about. The room had not been dusted in some time.

"What a mess," said Jasmin.

"It's almost the opposite of the rest of the house. I would not have expected this. Is that...is that a half-eaten sandwich there?"

On a plate, half covered by a *Home and Gardens* magazine was indeed an unfinished sandwich. Torie didn't even want to guess how long it had been there.

"Whatever smells so bad seems to be coming from the closet," said Jasmin, jutting her chin in that direction.

"Maybe it's just more rotting food. I honestly wouldn't be surprised."

This time, as they approached the door, Jasmin reached for the handle while Torie summoned her magic and held it at the ready for whatever may be inside.

Pulling the door open, Jasmin jumped back to stand next to Torie as they both peered anxiously inside. This time, the smell of something rotten hit them in their physical senses as well as their mystical ones. It took quite a bit of willpower and magic to push it away from their minds as the two witches stumbled back.

After the initial shock of the exposure, they pushed forward, Torie feeling along the inside wall for a light switch. Not finding one, she cast a spell that created a floating globe of white light, illuminating the space. Inside the closet, half the space was dedicated to men's suits, while more casual wear took up shelving and rack space on the other side.

On the floor of the closet was a laundry bin that overflowed with unwashed clothing, and next to that was a shoe rack where the mayor's dress shoes sat alongside a couple of pairs of sneakers.

But other than that, the space was empty.

"There's nothing here," said Torie, still covering her mouth to guard against the stench.

"No, there definitely is something here."

Jasmin lifted a hand and closed her eyes. "There's a cloaking spell in place. I can feel it." She whispered an incantation that struck out at the barrier in front of them. The air rippled in response.

"Yes, I can feel it now," said Torie. "It's very strong."

"Help me break through," said Jasmin.

Together the witches placed their hands on the invisible wall and pushed their magic against it. The barrier flared red at the touch of their hex power, crackling in the air as it slowly gave in to their power and fell away.

Once it was gone, the wall behind it looked completely different. Gone was the clothing that was folded and placed on the built-in shelves, and in their place was a number of ornamental, heavily lacquered boxes. Each box was intricately gilded and locked with a tiny, golden lock.

"Well, what have we here?" said Jasmin, taking one of the boxes from the shelf. In all they counted seven boxes, all roughly the same dimensions; measuring about two feet square.

The box she carried was emerald green with gold trim and a curved front. It had four ornately carved legs and she sat it on the bed before them. A lot of work had gone into making them and there was no telling what price tag, if any, could be placed on them.

"The same magic that created the shielding spell is

protecting these as well," Jasmin said. "Only more concentrated. It could take us all day looking through this pig pen to find the physical key for them."

"Even if we did find the key, I'm betting it would be useless without the spell to drop the shielding."

"Well then, I guess it's a good thing we are witches. We will simply have to undo the shielding ourselves. Divide and conquer?"

Torie nodded, focusing her attention on the box.

The technique they used was one that Jasmin had only recently taught her. It involved the two of them performing two different magical chants simultaneously. The idea was that the magic shield could ward off one form of their hex magic, but it would not be able to withstand dual attacks of two different magical incantations.

Their voices rose in pitch as they called on their hex power to break through the enchantment that protected the box. Resistance was strong; stronger than they were expecting. Beads of sweat broke out on the two witches' foreheads as they continued to call on their power. They sensed the wards begin to weaken and upped the ante, applying even more hex power.

Finally, the gold lock popped open and dropped to the bed.

"Whew. That was harder than it should have been," said Jasmin.

She gave Torie one last look before slowly opening the lid on the box. They both peered inside in horror at what they found.

Inside, resting on a silk cushion, was what looked like a large, red and gray heart of some kind. It was bigger than a human heart, but the general shape of it let them know that it belonged to something whose physiology wasn't too far away from their own.

There were no cuts to the vessels and valves that extended from the chambers. Rather, the ends were ragged and ill formed. It had been ripped out of something savagely and then placed in the box.

Despite her horror, Torie bent closer to examine it.

"Wait. Please tell me that is not..." She used her magic to float the heart up out of the box and turn it slightly in midair so they could see the underside more clearly. There were what looked like teeth marks along the bottom where it rested in the box. In disgust, she placed it back into the box and looked away.

"Well, at least we know what that smell is," Jasmin said, nodding at the closet. "God knows what's in the rest of those."

"Well, she may know, but we need to know as well. But not here. We need to get these back to the house."

"Wait, you want to bring this to my house?" She wrinkled her nose in disgust.

"I don't think we want anyone else finding these. Plus, whatever is going on is a lot darker than I was thinking. There is strength in numbers, and it will take us working together to unlock the rest of these."

"What about that shadow we sensed earlier? It's still here."

"And I'm betting that it is tied to these boxes somehow. We can come back and cleanse this place later. But this is definitely looking like something that can help absolve you of any involvement."

Reluctantly, Torie agreed. She wasn't keen on the thought of desecrating her new house with a ripped-out animal heart and who knows what else; but she also knew that something that radiated so much darkness wasn't good to be left unattended.

Things like this tended to attract rather unsavory super-natural elements. She would have to trust that whatever came forward, she and Jasmin would be able to handle.

Closing the box, they started the laborious effort of carrying each box one at a time and placing it in the back of Jasmin's SUV.

Chapter Fifteen

The ride home was uneventful at least. Torie kept looking over her shoulder at their cargo, sending snippets of magic their way to probe them occasionally.

"Would you stop doing that?" said Jasmin. "They aren't going anywhere."

"I know. But they make me nervous sitting back there."

"Well, you're making me nervous. I say, all things considered, we should probably head straight back home. It would not be a good idea to stop in town at the market with these rattling around in the car."

Torie couldn't agree more. The sooner she was back in her home, even with boxes filled with what she could only assume were more stolen organs, the better she would feel. She felt like she needed a long, hot shower.

Make that a Silkwood shower, she thought.

Luckily, once they got back to the house, Elric was there waiting for them on the porch. Torie had texted him to be sure he would be available to help carry the boxes inside.

"What's up?" he asked. "Got your text. Did you find anything interesting at the mayor's?"

"You might say that," said Torie as Jasmin popped the tailgate on her car.

Elric looked at the gleaming boxes and let out a low whistle. "Can't wait to tease Max about how he missed all this in his sweep of the house."

"He wouldn't have found these. They were hidden with magic, magic that I'm betting thwarted even his senses, though I can't imagine how he missed that stench," said Jasmin. "Let's get these into the study."

Together, they moved the boxes into Torie's study, setting them on her long work desk in a row.

Leo bounded up to Torie happily and scampered up onto her shoulder. She immediately felt better. The stress of the last couple of hours started to melt away as she playfully scratched at the dragon's belly.

Fionna came into the room, curious what was going on.

"How's Effie?" asked Torie.

"Oh, she's fine. I've been going back and forth between her room and taking care of this little fella. You know, Effie thinks you have a cat, and she keeps asking to play with it."

Torie smiled. "Yeah, well this little cat doesn't seem to play so well with others."

"What have you got there?" asked Fionna, looking at the boxes. She reached for one, but Jasmin stopped her.

"I wouldn't," she said. "They are warded with magic and...well, we don't know what's inside." She gave Torie a quick look.

"Fionna, can you do me a favor and take Leo to another part of the house to entertain while we get these open? I'd rather he not be exposed to this. And you either for that matter."

"Sure, not a problem. Come here, you." She took him off Torie's shoulder and cradled him like a baby as she walked out of the study.

Elric frowned. "What was that about? You've never not let Fionna be around when you performed magic."

Torie looked at him and then Jasmin.

"There is something very dark going on at the mayor's house, and these boxes…well, they are filled with some pretty nasty stuff. At least the first one we opened was. It's probably not a good idea having anyone non-magical around when we open them. That includes you," Torie said, moving to stand next to Elric and caress his cheek.

"Yeah, well that pretty much means I'm not leaving. I might not be able to help open them, but I'll be here to help deal with whatever comes out if need be."

Torie knew not to argue. Elric was extremely protective of her, and it was truly one of the things that she enjoyed the most about him.

"Fine," said Jasmin, "but before we do anything, I think we need to not only raise wards of our own about the house, but we need to make doubly sure this room is sealed."

Torie agreed and asked Elric to take a seat at the far side of the room, away from the desk where the gilded boxes were.

She moved to the center of the room and raised both arms, activating the shields she and Jasmin had worked so hard to create. Then, taking Jasmin's hand, both witches began to chant.

"Oh Silver Lady, grant us this boon,
and let no evil escape this room."

While he wasn't sure what it was, Elric felt a wave emanate from the witches and pass through him. His supernatural senses were on high alert, and he decided to give in to the urge to shift into his wolf form. In that form, his senses were even sharper, and he immediately zeroed in on the boxes on the table. Torie was right. They reeked of darkness. He let out a little growl and stole down onto the floor, watching keenly as the witches began to use their magic to assault the tiny boxes.

As before, Torie and Jasmin worked in unison; first stripping away the magical shields that surrounded each box, before then attacking the tiny gold locks.

Again, their tactic was a success as one by one the locks popped open and then dropped away with a small thud to land on the desktop.

Elric rose to all fours and started to make his way over to the boxes, but Torie waved him off.

"Stay back," she said. "Just in case there is something in here that you shouldn't be exposed to."

They slowly began to open the boxes. Torie lifted each lid and Jasmin stood next to her, magic at the ready if needed. Once all the boxes had been opened, they took stock of what they had.

"Well, no booby traps at least," said Torie. "Seems like the shielding and the locks were all the protection placed on them."

"Gross. Why would anyone want to protect all that?" It was Elric, standing behind the witches and peering over their shoulder.

He was right. Torie looked at the contents in disgust. To go with the heart, there were more organs, some of which had come from humans, and some they had no clue as to what they were.

There were two kidneys, a black oily liver, a large tongue that looked far too big to belong to any human being, a complete brain that seemed to be the size of a golf ball, and an ear that was covered in fur. Those, along with the heart they had seen earlier, accounted for the contents of the boxes.

"This is black magic," said Jasmin. "Sacrificial magic of the darkest order. What in the name of all that is holy was the mayor into?"

"Elric, I hate to ask, but…what do they smell like to you? Can you tell what these are from?"

Elric shifted into his hybrid form. It allowed him to remain standing upright, but also gave him access to his more supernatural senses. He leaned forward and sniffed at the gory collection.

"No idea," he said, his voice guttural and deep. "Wherever these came from they've been here for a while. I can't pick up any trace scents other than the lingering death odor."

"Yes, they are old," said Jasmin. "But they aren't really decayed. Interesting."

Torie wasn't sure if interesting was the word she would have used.

"So, what do we do with them?" she asked.

"First, we call Max and see if he is willing to scrub your name from all involvement with this. Then, we start some research into just what is involved in this kind of sacrificial magic, and how it benefits humans. The mayor was into something alright. Something that got him killed."

"So do we leave them here?" asked Torie, wrinkling her nose.

"I'm afraid so. This room is reinforced with spell protection, so for now, it's probably the best place."

Torie nodded in agreement. She might not have liked it, but she agreed with the statement.

"Well, now you'll need to find a new place to keep Leo. The way he tackled that plate of raw meat you gave him for breakfast, I hate to think what would happen if he got these boxes open."

The mental image was enough to almost make Torie heave.

"I'm going to move him into the bedroom with me. If Effie's sister is coming to visit, I don't need him freaking out on yet another human."

Jasmin didn't say anything, but Torie noticed a slight change in her body language.

"What is it? What's wrong?"

"It's nothing," Jasmin started, before turning to face her friend. "You know, that dragon isn't a pet. You're forming a very close bond with something that…I don't know, that we don't know what will happen to. It's a wild creature, Torie."

"Leo isn't a wild creature. He's part of the supernatural world, just like we are. He might be a little fidgety around certain people, but how do you think someone would react that has never known of the existence of werewolves and one night saw Elric shift? They would probably react the same way."

Jasmin didn't say anything because her friend had a good point.

"That's true; but what I'm saying is, maybe he doesn't belong here. What if he has family that don't know where he is? Supernaturals are highly intelligent. If something out there is looking for him, eventually they'll find him. And then what?"

Now it was Torie's turn to be silent.

"You're right. And when the time comes, I will do the

right thing. You know that. But in the meantime, I would like him to be as comfortable as possible. So, he can move into my bedroom."

"Well, that should be fun," said Elric. "Will he be sleeping on the bed with us? Because you know, until this is all over, there is no way I'm leaving you here by yourself."

Torie smiled at her lover. "I would not have expected anything else."

They left the study and headed back into the main part of the house.

"I'm going to run back to my house to get a couple of books on sacrificial magic and black lore," said Jasmin. "Maybe there is something in it that will give us a clue as to what is going on."

"Alright. I'll…I don't know. I'll find something to do around here," said Torie. Her mind was focused on the recording from the mayor's phone, and she was anxious to play it back again. Why was her name the subject of a murder victim and a mystery woman? "Also, I want to be here when Max and Elion return."

Jasmin nodded and gave her friend's arm a squeeze as she walked out the door.

Once she was gone, Torie walked into the kitchen to make herself a cup of tea. She glanced out the window and saw Fionna playing in the yard with Leo. He might not be a pet but that certainly didn't stop Fionna from playing fetch with him.

Reaching into her pocket, she took the phone out and laid it on the island. She pressed the play button and listened to the recording yet again. When it finished playing, she listened again. Still no clue as to what they were talking about.

"Torie, is that my son's voice?"

She turned to see Effie standing in the middle of the kitchen.

"Effie, what are you doing out of bed?" As soon as she said it, she regretted the words.

"That's just what Terry used to say before he started locking me in my room." She was visibly upset, and Torie felt ashamed of herself for having any part in the sadness that was coming off the woman in waves.

"Effie, I am so sorry. I just meant that you aren't familiar with the layout of this house yet. You are welcome to go anywhere you want, but I don't want you hurting yourself."

The woman smiled nervously. "Thank you. But this house seems to be very open with large hallways and rooms that don't have too much furniture and things lying about."

"Well, yes, I only just moved in. No clutter is one of the benefits of a new house I suppose."

Effie paused, wringing her hands together before her. "You didn't answer my question. Was that my son's voice I heard?"

Torie took a deep breath. "Yes, Effie, it was. The police found this and were wondering if maybe it was a clue that could help them find out what happened to him. I...I was just listening because the police heard my name on the recording and wondered if I knew anything."

"They think you had something to do with my son's death?" Effie tilted her head toward Torie, the sadness gone from her face as her expression took on a more hardened look.

"I didn't. I swear I didn't. I've never even met your son before. I have no idea what he and that other woman were talking about."

"Oh, I believe you. I can tell when I'm being lied to." Something in her tone caught Torie's attention.

"Well, I am hopeful that if the police can identify that mystery woman on the recording, they can help solve your son's accident."

"Oh, that woman? That's no mystery. That's his cousin. She's Hattie's daughter. She's as mean as my son was. Those two are always conspiring and up to no good. Bad eggs from the moment they were born. They have a special resentment for witches, so that's probably why they were plotting about you."

Torie looked at her, mouth hanging open.

"You...know?"

"Of course I do. I've lived in this town my whole life. I knew what you were the minute I met you."

Chapter Sixteen

Before Torie could digest what Effie had just said, the back door opened and Fionna walked in. She was carrying Leo playfully in her arms, and as soon as she saw Effie, she held the dragon close. Leo saw Effie standing there in her nightgown and began to squirm and hiss.

"Oh, is that your cat again?" asked the older woman. "May I please pet him?" She held out her hand in Leo's general direction and took a small shuffling step towards them.

"Uh, maybe not just yet," said Torie, motioning for Fionna to take him back outside. "He takes a while to warm up to people."

"Of course. Finicky little beasts those cats are," said Effie.

Again, Torie noticed the difference in the older woman. While her steps were shuffling, she seemed far steadier than she had previously. The tremor in her arms was gone and there was something very alert in her eyes and features as she spoke. Torie made a mental note to have Glen come check her later in the day.

Fionna quickly darted back out the door, one arm around Leo's struggling body, her other hand over his snout, as tiny wisps of smoke could be seen escaping between her fingers.

"Effie, what else do you know about this town?" asked Torie. She walked over to the woman and gently took her arm, leading her to a seat at the kitchen island. "Would you like some tea? I was just about to have a cup."

"That sounds lovely, dear," she said, settling into her seat.

Torie poured two cups of steaming water and added two teabags. "I'm sorry, I only have Earl Grey, but I'll add a bit of lemon and honey if you'd like."

"Oh no thank you. I don't like to dilute anything I put into my body."

Torie paused at the woman's turn of phrase, but then slid the cup to Effie, watching as she slowly picked it up, placing one tentative fingertip into the brew to gauge how full the cup was before taking a sip.

"Oh, this is excellent, Torie."

Torie took a sip of her own tea before diving back into the topic that had left her momentarily speechless.

"So, Effie, what do you know about Singing Falls?"

"Well, I know the average yearly temperature, the shops that are tourist traps, and when it was founded, if that is what you mean."

Torie frowned. "No, that isn't what I meant. You said you knew I was a witch. What else do you know?"

"Oh that." Her tone sounded almost dismissive. "If you mean do I know that there are all kinds of creatures living here in town, walking around in human form, then yes, I know all about that. But they've always been nice to us here in town, so I was always of the mindset, live and let live."

That was good for Torie to hear, especially since her other houseguests consisted of a werewolf and a squirrel shifter.

"And it doesn't bother you? What I am?"

Effie took another sip, shaking her head. "Not at all, dear. Witches are people too, right? I mean, you're not like those half-human creatures."

There it was again. The tone that Torie had noticed that would sometimes sneak into the elder woman's voice.

"I'm sorry. I shouldn't say such things. I've lived here all my life and I love this town. It's been good to me. Just that lately, there seem to be so many half breed creatures."

"Half breed?" queried Torie, not liking the older woman's choice of words.

"You know; half human and half animal. At least that's how they were explained to me all those years ago."

"Well, that isn't exactly the truth. They are called shifters. They are members of the supernatural community that can change forms; from human form to whatever their animal shape may be."

"So…half and half."

Torie pursed her lips. "Well, the way you say it is kind of demeaning, I think. Like saying someone who is of two races is a…half-breed."

Now it was Effie who frowned. "But isn't that what they are?"

Torie wasn't about to wade into that and decided to change the subject, trying to hide her annoyance. "What can you tell me about your niece? The woman that your son was on the phone with?"

Effie huffed, and Torie was pretty sure that if her eyes

weren't milky gray, she would have seen them roll back into her head at the mention.

"Her name is Tilda. She is Hattie's daughter and only a year younger than my Terry. Growing up, they were always inseparable those two. Always together plotting something."

"So, you grew up with your sister? Here in Singing Falls?"

"Yes, that is correct. We were both born here. We both married young, probably too young. Nothing good came of those relationships, however, and they didn't last. I guess most people would say that if we hadn't gotten married neither of us would have had them kids. So some people might say that was a blessing. Some people.

"But anyway, we raised them here, doing the best we could. But those two were always up to no good. They were always so jealous, trying to fit in where they couldn't."

"What do you mean?"

"With the townsfolk. You know, if you see something every day long enough, and you constantly think it's better than you, eventually you start to want to be like it." She paused, sipping her coffee, her gray eyes peering far off into a black distance. "That was always Terry and Tilda. Wanting to be what they never could be. Most folks in town didn't know about all the supernaturals running around; but we did. We had a maid that was a half-bre— I'm sorry, shifter. She tried to hide it but one day we caught her, changing into a fox and slipping out the back to go play in the woods with her kind.

"When Hattie confronted her, she admitted to what she was. That was when we found out about more of their kind all over town. And the kids knew, because they were in school with some of the offspring of these...shifters. So they were exposed to it early on. And that was when the seeds of jealousy started to be sown in their hearts. They wanted to be able to turn into animals too, couldn't figure out why they couldn't. We told them it was because they weren't born to it; they were born from us and we were pure human.

"I think that was when they started to resent us for not being able to give them something no one should have."

Torie was shocked at what she was hearing. She had always seen the supernatural community and the humans of Singing Falls living together in harmony. Other than the few isolated incidents over the last few months, the town seemed to be nicely integrated. But what Effie was saying made her believe that there was an underlying current of distrust beneath the calm veneer.

"So, did your children ever act on their jealousy?"

"Oh, they tried. They'd bully some of the smaller children, but one time Tilda's smart mouth got her nipped by a coyote pup. You'd think that would have taught her a lesson, but no. You know what those two did after she got bit?

"They sat around in Tilda's room for a month, waiting to see if she'd turn to a coyote on the next full moon. Their plan was, if she changed, she was then going to bite Terry and make him one too."

Effie laughed at a memory that Torie found sad and unsettling.

"They had no idea how it worked. None of us did. Still, the older they got, the more disturbing their behavior became. They became obsessed with that part of the community. And when they were teens, that's when they discovered that witches lived among us, and that opened a whole new world to them.

"They figured they could learn magic and eventually find a way to turn into animals." She shook her head, recounting the tale. "That's when we knew it was time to take action. We didn't know anything about your kind. But Hattie found some of the books they were studying. Black conjuring; magic practices that would chill your soul. We decided the best thing to do would be to separate them. So Hattie moved out west with Tilda, and I stayed here with Terry. We hoped that would stop all the nonsense, and it did. For a while.

"Tilda was always the leader of the two of them, so without her influence, Terry got in line quick and let all that supernatural nonsense go. But then recently, before he locked me away, I would catch him on the phone whispering to someone late at night and I knew who it was. I confronted him, and that was when…well, that was what got me remanded to my room."

"I am so sorry, Effie. I can't imagine what you must have been through."

She shrugged. "It's a good test; being given more than we think we can handle."

"Effie, do you remember any more about what happened? What led your son to…do what he did with you? When we found you, you seemed rather out of it."

There was a glint to the older woman's eyes that told Torie she had indeed remembered something.

"Yes, my wits are coming back to me. I was so tired and hungry when you found me. But yes, now I remember. Terry was saying that he had found something. That he had a collection of some sort that would grant him everything he and Tilda could ever want. He just needed one more thing to make it complete."

Torie shivered, thinking of the contents of the gilded boxes.

"Do you know what that one thing was?"

Effie shook her head. "Not at all. Truth is, I didn't want to know. I wanted no part of it, and I told him as much. I told him I was going to call Hattie and tell her what was going on as well, and he became very upset at that. That was when he locked me in my room. I tried knocking on the door, constantly pleading with him to let me out. He was afraid that someone would hear me so one day he put me in my bed and read some weird words out of a book. That was the last thing I remember...until I woke up with you and your friends."

Torie was nodding. Somehow, the mayor had figured out a way to cast a spell and had used it to bound his own mother to her bed.

"Thank you, Effie. You've helped me a lot."

"Oh, it's no bother. I like having someone to talk to, and you've been so nice to me."

"Well, you're welcome and yes, I have to admit it's been nice having you to talk with as well. I miss that."

She stopped, her voice trailing off. It was the first time she had admitted to herself that the reason she liked having Effie around so much was because she reminded Torie of her own mother. She would give anything to be able to speak with her again, and the fact that the mayor had done this to his mother made Torie's blood boil.

"Well, Effie, I'm going to call my friend Jasmin with this news, and then I'm going to call Glen over to check on you. Is that okay?"

"You mean that nice lady doctor? Of course. I like her."

"Glen isn't a doctor, but she's great at what she does. She and Fionna make an amazing couple."

Effie's eyes grew wide in surprise. "Couple? As in...you mean they are...*together*?"

"Yes, and they are very happy."

Effie scrunched up her nose and her mouth twisted to one side. "Just be sure she wears gloves." She pushed her cup away and held out her arm. "Could you be so kind as to help me back to my room?"

Her remark had struck a nerve with Torie, but she didn't say anything. Effie was older and came from a different generation, she reminded herself. She could only imagine the changes the elder woman had been a part of in her lifetime. Some things were probably easier for her to accept. Still, she made a mental note to talk all this over with Jasmin.

She helped Effie back to her room, made sure she was comfortable, and headed back into the kitchen, her mind still processing all that she had been told.

The sun was high in the sky when she stepped out onto the patio. There wasn't a cloud in the sky, just a swath of blue as far as she could see. It was shaping up to be another perfect, Carolina day.

There was a commotion to her right, and she turned to see Leo giving playful chase to Fionna. She had shifted to her squirrel form, and the two of them were racing around the furniture playing what looked like a game of supernatural tag. She laughed as they raced up to her, Fionna shifting back to human. She stood next to Torie, bending over to place her hands on her knees as she caught her breath.

"This little guy has way more energy than I do," she said.

Leo sprinted up Torie's arm to rest on her shoulder, his tail whipping lazily about.

"Good job wearing him out. What say we go put him down in my room, and then see what's keeping Jasmin and Max."

Fionna agreed and they all went back into the house. Just as they were about to head to Torie's master suite, the front door opened at the same time they heard the garage door open. Jasmin walked in from the front and Max and Elion entered from the back.

"Finally," said Torie. "You're not going to believe what I found out."

"And you're not going to believe what we found," said Max. He greeted the women just as Elric came down the stairs to join them. "We found out what really happened to the mayor. He was definitely murdered. By a supernatural."

Chapter Seventeen

Before more could be said, Torie held a finger to her lips. She walked down the corridor to Effie's room and peeked in on the sleeping woman. Then, she eased the door closed and headed back to her guests.

"We have to keep it down. Effie has ears like a bat and knows a lot more about what's going on than we gave her credit for."

"What do you mean?" asked Jasmin. "How much more?"

"Well, she knows I'm a witch for one thing, and she knows about shifters living in the town for another."

No one said anything as they all headed into the large kitchen.

"Here, give me Leo," said Fionna, lifting him from Torie's shoulder. "I'm going to go and put him away. I have a sneaking suspicion that this conversation is about to take a turn I'm not anxious to hear."

She gave Elion a look that let him know she still was not comfortable in his presence before leaving the room.

"I don't think I will ever win that one over," said Elion.

"That one? You haven't won *this* one over yet," said Jasmin, giving him a steely glance. "But what were you able to find out about the mayor, and why do you think his killer was a member of the supernatural community?"

"I did not say the killer was a member of your community. I just said that they were a supernatural. The mayor was poisoned as we suspected. The residual amount in his tissue sample was one I recognized but have not come across in many centuries."

Something about the way he said 'tissue sample' made Torie's stomach turn over.

"So, what is it?" she asked.

"It is a derivative of the Colombian poisonous tree frog," said Elion. "They are beautiful animals that secrete a poison so lethal that it can kill an adult man almost instantly."

"So, you're saying he was killed by…a frog shifter?" said Elric.

"No. I said the poison is derived from the frog. But it has been greatly enhanced to do what it did to the mayor. It was a controlled dose that was time delayed in its action. The poison itself was far more powerful than what would occur in the frogs. It came from something that shares the frog's DNA structure but has evolved in a completely different manner. Plus, as I said, it was time delayed and targeted only to interact with the man's brain so as to appear he died of natural causes. That implies the manipulation of some form of magics."

No one said anything as the information Elion had just laid on them seeped in.

"Elion, were you able to determine how long the delay was?" asked Jasmin.

The vampire shook his head. "Not exactly. But judging from the way the toxin is breaking down, I would say it was injected into the mayor about twelve hours before his death."

"So, we are looking for someone with access to poison from a creature that we have no idea what it could be and the means to magically control it. Great," said Jasmin. "Where do we even start with that?"

"Well, maybe it ties in to what I found out," said Torie. "I found out who the mystery woman on the phone is. Her name is Tilda, and she is Effie's niece. She's the daughter of her sister, Hattie."

She let that sink in before continuing.

"And get this. She's a bad seed who is obsessed with magic and shifters."

"Whoa," said Jasmin, pulling up a seat. "Why don't you start from the beginning and tell us everything you learned."

Ten minutes later, Torie had relayed her conversation with Effie, minus certain parts relating to terms that the elder woman used for certain members of the community.

"Well, things just got a little more interesting," said Jasmin. "So, we're looking for the mayor's cousin. Do you think she is in town?"

"My guess is yes," said Max. "If they were planning something, then it makes sense."

"But if that were the case, why would she not have been with the mayor? From what Effie said, they were pretty much inseparable," answered Torie.

"First things first. We can't find her if we don't even know what she looks like. I don't remember seeing any family photos at all when we were at the mayor's, do you?" Jasmin looked to Torie.

"No, now that you mention it. But it's probably time that we tell everyone what we did find."

"Or it may be easier to just show them," said Jasmin, nodding towards the back corridor that led away from the guest suite.

Torie led everyone to her study and to the row of boxes that sat on her desk.

"You found some fancy boxes?" said Max.

Jasmin eyed the wolf as she walked over to the first box and flipped it open. She moved down the desk opening each in turn, watching as the group grew more and more disturbed with each reveal.

"That's disgusting," said Max. "And trust me, I've seen a lot of gross stuff…but who would keep something like this? And why doesn't it stink to high hell? I didn't smell this when I was at the mayor's house."

"Probably because these were warded with magic and it's acting as some kind of mystical preservative. It probably blocked your physical senses." said Torie.

"If these were acquired by magic, and it was the doing of the mayor, wouldn't the spell protecting them have been broken when he was killed?" asked Elric.

"Normally, yes. But if he didn't work the incantation alone…" said Jasmin.

"Tilda, his cousin," said Torie. "That has to be the answer. That would mean that she is in Singing Falls somewhere."

"This is, fascinating," said Elion, moving closer to the boxes to get a clearer look at the contents.

"According to what I've found out, there are various reasons for sacrificial magic. It's a very old art form, and almost always involved the invocation of dark deities. Even though the practitioners may sometimes pray to a being of light, asking for their favor, it almost always ended in something from the world of black spirits that answered them," said Jasmin.

"True," said Elion. "But there are other reasons to perform these rituals. It wasn't always done to procure favor."

"Do you know if these are from humans or animals?" asked Max.

"Or something other," said Elion, half to himself and half aloud.

"No, we couldn't tell," said Jasmin, turning to Elion, "and what do you mean 'other'?"

"This one," he said, peering closely at the heart that was in the very first box Jasmin and Torie had opened. "This is extremely rare and unique I believe. The scent from it is almost intoxicating."

"What scent? I can't smell anything," said Max.

"That's because you're a werewolf. Your senses are a fraction of mine," replied the vampire.

Quickly, before they could stop him, he reached into the box, lifted the large heart to his mouth and bit into it as casually as if it were an apple.

He ignored the gasps of disgust that came from everyone around him and instead closed his eyes and concentrated on the feel of the chewy flesh his fangs had just penetrated. He placed the heart back into the box, black blood leaking from the two puncture sites he had inflicted.

"As I suspected," he said, wiping his lips with the back of his hand. "That is a dragon's heart."

No one said a word, their minds spinning in all directions.

"Are...are you sure?" asked Torie.

"Quite sure. The tang of the blood is rapturous and unique."

"Do I even want to know how you know what dragon blood tastes like?" asked Jasmin.

"Probably not. Would you like me to identify the rest of these?"

"Not now," said Torie. She needed to digest what he had just told her.

"Okay, now things are just getting more and more weird," said Jasmin. "On top of everything else, you find a baby dragon at your front door, and now we find out that a dragon was part of a black magic ritual? I would say it's coincidence, but you know I don't believe in those."

Torie had to admit that this was too close to be a coincidence, as much as she may have hoped otherwise.

"So where does this leave us?" she questioned.

"Well, I know where that leaves me," said Max. "I'm going to cancel the festival for this year. The mayor's murder is one thing, but add the rest of this, and I'm not willing to risk any other members of the community getting killed until we can figure out what is going on."

Before they could object, Fionna stormed into the room, her face red and her fists clenched.

"Fionna, what's wrong, what happened?" asked Torie.

"I just checked in on Effie to see if she needed anything, and she told me that she was feeling a little hungry but that if I made her food, I needed to be sure and put on gloves. After all, she doesn't want to catch anything that my kind may spread around." She crossed her arms, staring at Torie. "Somehow, I don't think she meant squirrel-shifter."

Torie felt herself blush.

"You're right. I told her about you and Glen in passing...I didn't think anything at all about it."

149

"Well, she obviously did."

Jasmin looked over at Torie, the look in her eyes saying more than her words ever would.

"I know, I know…" said Torie. "She does have some bigoted beliefs. But I don't think she means anything bad by it. She's old and grew up here in the south. She is going to have certain…views on things."

"I'm old and I grew up here in the south," said Jasmin. "I'd never in a million years think such things about anyone. And neither do you, Torie, so why are you letting her get away with whatever crap she's been saying?"

"I called her out on it; I explained why she shouldn't say such things, but it obviously didn't stick with her."

"Well, you can get her some food," said Fionna. "I'm not going back in there. Just wait till I tell Glen."

Torie started to say something but was interrupted by the ringing of the doorbell accompanied by the alert coming from the computer monitor on her desk. She clicked a button and the security feed displayed the image of an older woman with a brown duffel bag standing on her porch.

"Hello, can I help you?" Torie said into the computer.

"Yes, my name is Hattie Stanor and I'm here to see my sister, Effie."

Chapter Eighteen

"Ms. Stanor, it is so nice to meet you," said Torie, extending her hand as she opened the door. "My name is Torie, we spoke on the phone."

"Please, it's Hattie. And thank you so much for calling me. For taking my sister in like this."

Torie took her bag and ushered her into the great room.

"Hattie, these are my friends. Fionna, Jasmin, Elric, Max and Elion."

"Well, it's nice to meet you all. So many faces and names. You know I won't be able to remember them all I'm afraid."

Torie smiled. "No problem. There won't be a quiz afterwards."

Hattie frowned, not quite sure what Torie meant.

"It's nothing. Just a bad joke. I wasn't aware you would be able to get here so quickly."

"Oh, I got on the very next flight out here as soon as I hung up from speaking with you."

"Well, you must be exhausted. Can I get you something to eat or drink? Some water maybe?"

"No, I am fine. Can I please see Effie?"

"Absolutely, of course. Come on, she's in the guest room down the hall."

Torie led her, followed by Jasmin and Fionna, to the guest room. Elric and Max had decided to hang back so as not to intrude.

"Would you mind if I go and...examine the rest of your artifacts?" asked Elion.

"Knock yourself out," Torie had whispered back to him.

At the door to Effie's room, Torie knocked lightly before pushing it open. "Effie, I have a surprise for you."

Torie entered the room with Hattie trailing close behind her.

"Effie?" said Hattie. "Oh, Effie, my sweet, sweet sister."

Effie's eyes lit up as she sat bolt upright in bed, throwing her arms wide for her sister to fall into her embrace.

"Hattie, is it really you?" asked Effie, rocking her sister in her arms.

Tears flowed from both women as they embraced one another as tightly as they could. Finally, Hattie broke free long enough to grasp Effie by her face.

"Let me get a look at you, sister," she said. "You look good. I see these women are taking good care of you."

"Oh, they are so nice," said Effie. "Torie is one of the women who found me and brought me here to rest. Did you meet her? She has a friend Jasmin that is just so funny, and her other friend Fionna is just the nicest girl. Even though she likes other women, she is still a nice person. I'm sad that such a nice person is going to go to hell."

Torie heard Fionna huff as she turned her back and stormed down the hall.

Jasmin shook her head, staring at Torie.

"Now, Effie, we talked about that. We don't judge," said Hattie, embracing her once again.

"Oh, you've spent too much time out with all those hippies buying into that stuff," said Effie. "But I am so happy you're here. Are we going home now? Can we go back to my house? Oh, Hattie, do you know what happened to Terry? It's awful. I'm all alone now."

Hattie looked at Torie and Jasmin questioningly.

"Well, I think that's something we need to discuss," said Hattie. "What do you think?"

"Well, I was going to have my friend Glen come and check her out. She is the one that has helped to take care of her medical issues."

"She's the lady doctor that is involved with Fionna," said Effie. "She's nice but is also going to go to hell."

"Hush with all that," said Hattie. "What does this doctor friend of yours say?"

"She isn't a doctor. She's a nurse, but she is very good, and well qualified. If you'd like we can certainly reach out to a physician to check over her," said Jasmin. Her words said one thing, but her tone told them that she would be just as happy not having Glen waste more of her time with the elder woman.

Torie gave her a look, and Jasmin merely shrugged in response.

"Oh no, that's quite alright," said Hattie. "She seems fine, and I can certainly look after her."

"Um, okay, that's fine," said Torie, "but there are a couple of things I think we should discuss. But maybe in the other room?"

Effie spoke up. "If you're going to tell her you're a witch that's not a big deal."

Torie smiled. "Well, that's good to know. But there are other things as well. We will be back soon. You just rest here for a bit."

Hattie gave her sister's hand a squeeze and leaned in to kiss her on the forehead. "I'll be right back. Just give me a second."

Together they left the room and headed back to the kitchen. "I apologize for my sister's words. She means well but is pretty set in her ways."

Jasmin didn't say anything, instead moved to make some tea.

"Would you like some?" she said to Hattie.

"No, thank you. But I will have some water, if that's okay?"

Torie went to the refrigerator and took out a bottle of water and offered it to her guest. This was the first time she had really focused on Hattie, and she was shocked to find that the woman looked nearly identical to her sister. Her skin was a deeper, dusky tan from years of being exposed to the weather. Fine lines etched into her features around her lips and eyes were especially noticeable due to the fact she wore no makeup. Her hair was long and brushed back; Torie could tell that at one point it had been a dark chestnut color, but now it was mostly gray. It reminded Torie of the streak in her own hair that she had tried so desperately to remove.

Torie admired the fact that she chose not to cover up the features that showed she had lived life and wasn't ashamed of it. She had to be in her late sixties, but you would never have known it based on the way she moved as she hopped onto the bar chair and threw back her water.

"Hattie, how much do you know about what Effie's son may have been up to?"

"Well, I'm sure whatever he was doing it was no good," she replied disgustedly.

Torie exchanged glances with Jasmin, trying to decide how much to tell her.

"Are you aware that he had your mother locked in her bedroom? Basically restrained to her bed?" asked Jasmin.

Hattie started, nearly dropping her water bottle. "I knew he wouldn't let her call me, but I had no idea he had taken things that far. Why would he do that?"

"We don't know. We were hoping that maybe you could help shed some light on that," continued Jasmin.

"Are you aware he was practicing black magic?" asked Torie.

Hattie had a look of disgust on her face. "No, but I'm not surprised. I'm sure that is what got him killed. Is that what you're getting at?"

"What about your daughter? Do you know where she is?" asked Jasmin.

"Tilda? No, I haven't seen her in almost a year. Do you think she had something to do with this?"

"It's just that, Effie told us the two of them were inseparable. If she's here in Singing Falls and was with Terry, she might know something," said Torie.

"We aren't saying she had anything to do with it, but if she was with him and knows something, she might be in danger as well. We are pretty sure your nephew was murdered."

Hattie shook her head. A great sadness clouded her features as she looked at the two women.

"My daughter had a falling out with Terry about something. I don't know what it was because she stopped speaking to me. But I'm sure she didn't have anything to do with his death. She really is not a bad person, and neither is Terry. It's just that when they are together, bad things tend to happen. That was why I moved so far away from Effie and took Tilda with me all those years ago when she was young. We thought, if we could just let them grow up apart, maybe, just maybe, they would turn out to be the good people we knew they could be. But I see that isn't the case."

A single tear rolled down her cheek, and Torie quickly moved to get her a tissue. Hattie dabbed at her eyes, fighting to control the flood of tears that Torie sensed she was only seconds away from.

"Hattie, do you have a recent picture of your daughter? Or maybe even a personal effect of hers? We need to speak with her, and to do that we need to find her."

Hattie thought for a moment. "Well, I do keep a picture of her with me at all times. It's in my bag. But something personal? I'm not sure I have anything like that."

Torie went into the great room and retrieved her duffel bag, sitting it on the island in front of her.

Hattie dug around in it, pulling out a myriad of items— two bags of hard candies, Chapstick, a couple of pill bottles —before she removed a small wallet-sized purse. She opened it and took out a small picture of a smiling woman with red hair and hazel eyes.

"Here, this is Tilda," she said, handing the picture over to Torie. As she leaned across the island, something sparkled in the light streaming through the windows.

"Hattie, that is a lovely ring you're wearing around your neck," said Jasmin.

"Oh this," she said, reaching for the gold chain from which a silver ring with a topaz rhinestone dangled. "I forget about it sometimes. It was Tilda's. I wear it to try and keep her close to me even when she isn't around." Her eyes went wide at her words. "Do you think this would work for your personal artifact?"

Jasmin smiled, looking at Torie. "I think that will work just fine. May we borrow it?"

Tilda nodded and slipped the necklace over her head, handing it over to them.

"Are you going to cast some kind of witch spell on it to find my Tilda?" she asked.

Jasmin seemed nervous about the question but answered her truthfully.

"Something like that. This will certainly help us."

Just then, Elric and Elion walked into the room with Max trailing behind them, head down, scribbling in his notepad.

"I think we found out what we needed from the—" Elric started, but caught himself when he saw Hattie sitting there, "—the items you were able to procure."

"Are they local?" asked Jasmin, fixing him with a stare.

"Absolutely," said Elric. "Except for that first big ticket item, the rest are almost definitely local and belong to certain citizens of Singing Falls."

"Also, with the exception of the one, they were all procured recently," added Max.

"Okay, well that is good to know," said Jasmin. "I guess that means our collector is still in the area, and I think Torie and I can pay them a call soon."

Elric turned to face Torie. "I'll go change and will accompany you."

"No, that's okay," said Torie. "I appreciate the concern, but this is something that Jasmin and I need to do. Why don't you stay here and see to our guests? Or, better yet, I left a list in my study of items I need for Fionna's party. Maybe you can go pick those up."

Elric wrinkled his nose and gave her a questioning look. Torie jerked her head towards the patio door, and both of them stepped outside.

"Look, I appreciate you wanting to do this, really I do, but I'm not helpless. My magic is stronger than ever and whatever is going on here definitely requires magic. I'll feel better knowing you are here watching over Effie and Hattie. Whatever else is going on, it seems to revolve around their children. One has already been murdered and it looks like the other is elbows deep in that killing. Someone needs to stay with them, and I don't fully trust Elion to do that. He's always wanting to bite stuff, and I don't like the way he looks at Effie."

"I don't like it...but fine. I will do as you ask."

She gave him a quick kiss and turned to go back inside.

They closed the door behind them, just as Fionna came tearing into the room, chasing after Leo. The dragon roared as it scampered full speed at Hattie. Before it could reach her, Elion, moving faster than their eyes could follow, scooped him up and cradled him in a grip that the young dragon had no chance of escaping.

"Oh my," said Hattie, eyes focused on the dragon. "What an interesting cat that is. Wherever did you get one with such markings?"

No one said anything as they all looked from Hattie to the dragon and back to Hattie again.

"A...cat?" said Torie. "You can see the cat?" Then she shook her head, smiling. "What am I saying; of course you can see the cat. The cat that Elion is holding."

"Yes," said Hattie, "that cat. Looks like he's a feisty one!"

"Yes, he is still getting accustomed to the new house. Elion, you and Fionna take little Leo back upstairs for a bit so he doesn't get too worked up?"

Fionna looked at Elion and frowned but nodded her head.

"Happy to," she said, forcing a smile and waving Elion on ahead of her.

"Elric, why don't you show Hattie back to the guest room with Effie while Jasmin and I run the errand we discussed. We should be back shortly."

Elric nodded without saying anything.

Torie took the picture of Tilda she had out of her pocket and handed it to Max.

"Max, take this into town and see if anyone has seen Hattie's daughter. Maybe we'll get lucky. Jasmin and I will check with some other sources we have." She gave the sheriff a nod and then watched as the big werewolf headed out the door.

"Hattie, Elric is going to take you back to Effie. Glen, the nurse, will be here soon to check over her. If you need anything at all, just let Elric know."

Once everyone had cleared out of the kitchen, Jasmin gave Torie a long, appreciative look.

"What?" asked Torie.

"Nothing, just enjoying watching you take charge like that."

Torie blushed. She had never been good at taking compliments and quickly steered the conversation away from anything that had to do with her.

"So, we have a ring that Tilda wore, are you thinking a locator spell?"

Jasmin nodded. "Exactly. But we can't cast it from here. Between the wards you have, and those awful boxes in your study, the residual supernatural energy in this place could throw off the accuracy. We need calm. Let's go up to my place and see if we can't find this Tilda."

Torie agreed and followed her friend as they headed out of the house. She closed the door, and instinctively went to raise the wards around it, but then thought better. With all the comings and goings of supernaturals, it would be better to just leave them down. After all, they would only be away for a short time.

What was the worst that could happen?

Chapter Nineteen

"You know that was hurtful to Fionna, right?" said Jasmin as she opened the door to her house.

Torie couldn't look her in the eye because they both knew she was right.

"It was bad enough that Effie said those things, but it was even worse that I defended them without even meaning to," Torie replied. "I should have shut that down immediately. I thought I did...but I also didn't want to be forceful about it."

Jasmin turned to face her friend, her features softening. "Fionna knows you have her back. She also knows you can't control what comes out of someone else's mouth. Despite how she can sometimes appear outwardly, I think she can still be hurt by certain things; and this was one of them."

Torie didn't ask if the hurt was from Effie or Torie, and in truth, it didn't matter. She needed to make amends with her friend, and she intended to do so as soon as she returned to her own house. But just then, in that moment, she knew that she had to banish all distractions from her mind. She and Jasmin had work to do, and any stray thoughts could throw off the hex spell they were about to cast.

Like Torie, Jasmin had her own study that was located on the backside of her house, overlooking the manicured lawn. It was filled to overflowing with plants of all kinds that created an intoxicating aroma inside the room. Floor-to-ceiling bookcases were on every wall, including flanking the large picture window, and they were crammed full of tomes of all shapes and sizes.

"Have you read all of these?" asked Torie.

"Every single one of them. Reading is one of life's great pleasures, and a particular indulgence of mine. One day, if you don't hear from me, I'll probably have been crushed to death by an avalanche of books. And when you find me like that, just know that I died happy."

Torie rolled her eyes. "No talk of dying, young lady. We have so much more to do. And you have so much more to teach me."

"Not as much as you might think. You've come a long way in a very short period of time Torie. I'm starting to think you might be some kind of magical savant."

Torie shifted, looking away from her friend.

"Don't do that," said Jasmin.

"Do what?"

"Get all uncomfortable and change the subject when someone gives you a compliment. You earned that phrase. Accept it."

She started to protest but realized Jasmin was right. It was something she wanted to work on, and this was the perfect opportunity to do that.

"Thank you. You're right. I'm not good at taking compliments; it's something I'm not used to hearing. But you make it easy to learn and grow. Plus, it's something I feel like I'm really good at."

Jasmin smiled and nodded. "You're good at a lot of things, but you'll start to see that for yourself soon I'm betting. For now, let's find this Tilda person and see just what she's up to."

She went to one of the bookshelves on her wall and removed an old map that had been rolled into a tube and secured with a red ribbon. She placed it on a large work-table in the center of the room and unfurled the large piece of paper.

"What is that?"

"It's an old map of Singing Falls. Not much has changed with the town since its printing, so hopefully with the right spell we can locate Tilda."

"Why do you have paper maps? You know Google maps exist, right?"

"I know a lot of things exist, that doesn't mean I'm going to ditch the things I love for them. Besides, magic and technology aren't the best of friends for some reason. At least not at the level we need this spell to work."

Once the map was opened, she placed four small votives at each corner to keep it flat.

"Do you have the ring?"

"Right here," Torie replied, fishing it out of her pocket and handing it to Jasmin.

Holding the chain so the ring dangled over the map, Jasmin began to chant.

"From deepest cavern to highest peak,
show us now the one we seek."

Her eyes blazed white as she poured her intention and

power into the spell, and slowly, the ring began to swing about. It rotated in an ever-widening circle around the map, homing in on the object of their desire.

Faster and faster the ring swung, until, all at once, it stopped, pulling through the air at an angle that pointed at one area of the map. Jasmin released the chain and it zipped through the air to stick to one point on the map.

"Where is that?" asked Torie, peering closely at the area where the ring landed. "It looks like a campground at the base of the falls."

"It is," said Jasmin. "There is nothing there except RVs and small camping cabins. A lot of people come up from Queen City for the weekends to get away from everything. She may be holed up in one of them. It would be the perfect place to stay off the grid."

"Should we go take a look?"

"We should call Max, let that wolf earn his paycheck. But…"

"I did promise Elric I wouldn't go rushing headlong into things like this anymore without him. I just think he's probably needed more keeping the peace at the house than he will be of use to us."

"True. It's not like we are facing a hunter, or a crazed warlock that we would need his help in defeating. It's one human girl playing around with forces she shouldn't be. That's our wheelhouse."

Torie nodded in agreement. "You're right. We can handle this."

She smiled, realizing the ease with which they had talked themselves into something.

They headed out of the study, but Torie stopped in her tracks, leaning over to smell a particular flower with deep green stems and bright orange blooms that gave off a very fragrant scent.

"Jasmin, what is this?"

"It's an angel's trumpet. Specifically, a Brugmansia angel's trumpet."

"It smells amazing. Is it poisonous?"

"Yes, very. Well, the most dangerous part is in the seeds. This particular one I have been working on to breed out the poison so I can use the blossoms in healing potions." She gestured around the room. "All of these have been subjected to spell and incantation to create new forms that I can then adapt in various ways."

"Very impressive. I didn't know you had such a green thumb."

"Modern potions for the modern witch. No more eye of newt and tongue of frog for us. Why do you ask?"

"Oh, it just gives me an idea for something I am working on."

Together, they left Jasmin's house and piled into her black SUV and headed west, out of town.

"You know, she isn't your mother," said Jasmin, not taking her eyes off the road.

Torie didn't say anything, just turned her head to the side to gaze out her window.

"I know." She took a deep breath and released it on the windowpane, fogging it up. Then she traced a heart in her breath and slashed her finger through it before it faded away.

They were greeted by a large wooden archway with a sign that read 'Welcome to Camp Singing Falls' in large gold block lettering. Driving under the sign, they headed up a long, winding gravel road that led to an old country farmhouse. A sign suspended from small chains hung above the door and proclaimed this to be the rental office.

The two of them tried the door and found it unlocked. Inside the entry to the farmhouse had been carved up to create a small check-in desk to the right, and a tiny general store to the left that had a couple rows of stocked items that included mosquito spray, toiletries, canned goods, and camping supplies.

The house smelled old, but not in an unpleasant way; it reminded Torie of the smell of a large bookstore. Old paper was a scent she used to love, and it brought back so many fond memories of a time before she had purchased her first Kindle reading device and abandoned bookstores without a second thought.

A middle-aged man looked up from a crossword puzzle he had been working on and smiled as they approached him.

"Hello, ladies, what can I do you for?" he asked. "If you're looking for a cabin, I'm afraid we're all booked up, but I can check and see if anyone has cancelled for you." He made a move towards a large, boxy computer monitor but Jasmin stopped him.

"No, no, we aren't here for a cabin. We don't want to take up your time, but we are looking for someone. Have you seen this woman?"

She stepped aside and Torie walked up to the counter and took out her phone. She had snapped a picture of the photo of Tilda before giving it to Max.

The man looked at it, adjusting his glasses a bit.

"No," he said, with just a bit of hesitation. "Haven't seen anyone that looks like that here." Again, he turned away and looked at his monitor. "Well, will you look at that. Seems like we had a cancellation, but someone just booked it online. Looks like we really don't have anything here for you ladies."

Torie smiled and nodded.

"Well, thank you for your time, sir. I guess we'll be going now."

He nodded curtly and went back to his crossword puzzle as they walked out the door and stepped onto the creaking front porch.

"What do you think?" asked Jasmin.

"He was lying. I didn't even need magic to realize that. So now what?"

"Well, he'll probably be watching to see that we leave, so let's pull the car back down the hill a ways, and then we'll just go for a little walk in these lovely hills. If we just happen to cross back onto the property where the cabins are…well, we're just a couple of city girls out for a hike and didn't realize just how easy it is to get lost around here."

Torie smiled and nodded as they headed back for the car.

"See, this is yet another reason that we couldn't have sent Max in any official capacity. I'm sure he would not be able to trespass and continue a search after being told she wasn't here."

"Hey, we aren't trespassing. We're hiking."

Torie laughed as the big SUV headed back down the drive and exited the campground. Jasmin eased the vehicle off the road onto the shoulder once they were around a slight bend and out of sight of any part of the campground.

"Well, it's a good thing I wore my sensible shoes," Jasmin said, lifting one leg to show off her athletic attire.

"Like you wear anything else," said Torie. "One of these days we are going to get you into a pair of heels."

"Yeah, good luck with that. I will not be that woman from the movies who is getting chased by something and just falls down because of her shoes. Not that I'm going to be running from anything, but you get the idea."

Torie shook her head good-naturedly, and together they made their way into the overgrown thickets that led to a dirt path through the trees. The sunlight breaking through the canopy created long shadows that stretched before them; acting as a reminder that the afternoon was passing quickly into evening.

The thought that their pretend lost story could become all too real if they were caught out after sunset flashed briefly through Torie's mind.

"This looks like a pretty large campsite," she said. "How do we find Tilda?"

"Way ahead of you on that one." Jasmin reached into her pocket and withdrew the necklace they had used to find Tilda's location. "This is already enchanted to find her. All I have to do now is give it a little nudge."

She held the chain and ring in the palm of her hand and whispered to the piece of jewelry.

"*Alliz allim attredes*," she said, wrapping the ring in her spell. The ring and the chain began to glow with blue light as it lifted out of her hand and began to float ahead of them along the path.

"Does it know to stay away from people if possible?" asked Torie.

"Do I look like an amateur? It will seek out its owner, but it won't lead us through humans. All we have to do is follow it."

Thirty minutes later, Torie was wishing she had bought

some of that mosquito spray from the general store when they finally broke through some brush to a small, one-room cabin sitting off by itself near the back of the trail. The glowing ring headed directly for it, but Jasmin waved her hand and recalled it.

Placing the necklace back in her pocket, she nodded towards the cabin. "That's it."

Together, they made their way towards the cabin. The wooden door was closed and a single light bulb was the only indication that there was electricity running to the simple unit. There was parking space to the side for a camper or two cars, that was empty.

Torie stretched out her hand, feeling for any potential magical wards or booby trap.

"Nothing," she said. "Shall we?"

Jasmin nodded and the two of them stepped up onto the porch. Torie reached for the doorknob only to have the door swing open before she could touch it.

The red-haired woman that opened the door stepped back and held up a black gemstone before her. She screamed at the two women and the stone flared to life, striking them with a bolt of light.

Chapter Twenty

The witches were momentarily blinded by the light and both raised an arm to shield their eyes. Torie stumbled and was reminded what it felt like when she was a child and her mother used to take polaroid snapshots of her with that awful light strip attached to it.

Just as quickly as it hit them, it was gone, and the world slowly came back into focus. Torie blinked away floating specks of silver that wafted across her field of vision and could see the frightened woman in the cabin had taken a few steps back. Her eyes were wide at the sight of them, and again she held the stone up in front of her to try and blind them yet again.

"Nope, not this time," said Torie, holding out her hand. She focused her own magic and called to the stone. "Shiny gem," and it instantly flew across the room to land in her hand.

"Tilda, is that you?" asked Jasmin, still blinking away the light.

The sound of her name seemed to frighten the woman

even more. This time, she dug into a small bag she had strapped obliquely across her body. She hauled out a handful of white powder and blew it in the direction of the witches.

Jasmin waved her hand, sending a wave of blue light at the powder and incinerating it midair. Torie again held out her hand and this time summoned the bag from the woman. The strap broke as it flew over to the witch.

"*Infernis*," Torie said, causing the bag and whatever else may have been hiding in it to burst into flames.

"Tilda, we aren't here to fight. And as you can see, your little parlor tricks are pretty much useless against us, so if you have anything else up your sleeve, you might want to think twice before trying it," said Jasmin.

The woman's shoulders slouched.

"I don't have anything else," she said. "So go ahead, get it over with. Just make it quick please."

Torie and Jasmin exchanged quick looks.

"What are you talking about? Get what over with?" asked Torie.

"Kill me," said Tilda. "I assume that's what you're here for. To finish the job and take me out the way you did my cousin."

Torie held up both hands, simultaneously asking her to slow down while trying to reassure her that they meant no harm.

"I promise you, no one is here trying to kill you. We just want to ask you some questions, that's all."

There was a single bed on one wall of the cabin and a set of single bunk beds on the other. That, along with a couple of outlets on the wall, comprised the entirety of the cabin. Tilda had a small, red messenger bag and a matching overnight bag that she had thrown onto the foot of the single bed. She plopped herself down on the bed, nervously watching the two witches that stood only feet from her.

"You're witches. How am I supposed to know you're telling the truth?" she said.

"Because we have no reason to lie to you," said Jasmin. "We are just here trying to find out what happened to the mayor, your cousin."

"Where did you learn those protection spells you were throwing at us?" asked Torie.

"From a book I stole from my mom's library. It's pretty basic as you saw, but it was all I had."

"You shouldn't be playing with magic," said Jasmin as she probed around the room for any other surprises.

The woman huffed and looked away. "That's easy for you to say. How did you find me anyway?"

Jasmin took the necklace and ring out of her pocket and tossed it to her. "Magic, of course."

"Mom. I should have known. Birds of a feather after all…" Tilda said.

"What are you talking about?" asked Jasmin, but the woman remained quiet, still not looking them in the eyes.

"Look, let's just cut to the chase, did you kill Terry?" questioned Torie.

"No," she replied, looking up in shock. Her reply was immediate and the look on her face told them she wasn't lying. "Are you going to try and pin that on me?"

"No, we aren't. But it's what we came here to find out," said Jasmin.

Tears suddenly flowed down Tilda's face and she wiped them away with the palm of her hand. "How did he die?"

"You…you don't know?" asked Torie.

Tilda shook her head. "We had hourly check-ins and

when he didn't call after he had made plans to go see you, I figured he was dead."

"You know who we are?"

"Of course I do. Two of the most powerful witches in Singing Falls. I warned Terry not to go to you, but he said it was our only shot. Look where that got him." She started crying again, this time reaching for her overnight bag where she removed a few tissues to dab at her face.

Torie moved over to sit on the bed next to her. "Tilda, I am sorry about your cousin. He was poisoned, by a very rare and deadly type of magical poison that we haven't yet been able to identify."

Tilda sat up straight. "Magical poison? But you didn't do it?"

"No, I've never even met your cousin before. Why was he coming to see me the day he died?"

"Because we were at our wits' end and didn't know where to turn to for help. He said we needed help from a witch. A real witch that could do things that we couldn't learn from reading books. He said that everything he had heard about you was that you were kind and generous; the opposite of what we were told."

"What were you told about me?"

"That like all witches, you only wanted more and more power and that you increased your power through sacrificing babies and children. That was the source for all witches' powers."

Torie's mouth dropped open in shock as she looked at Jasmin.

"Tilda, none of that is true," said Jasmin. "Who told you such nonsense?"

"My mother. She said that's why you never see witches with children, because you use them as sacrifices and that you would kill anyone that ever found out your secrets. That was why we were never allowed to talk about it to anyone outside of Singing Falls. It was this town's ugly secret, Mom used to say."

Torie was shaking her head in disbelief. "That is nonsense. Why would anyone tell that to children? I would never hurt an innocent and neither would Jasmin."

Tilda sniffed hard. "That's what Terry thought; what he had heard about you. That was why he was going to you for help."

"Help with what?" asked Torie.

"Help stopping our parents. They had done some very bad things…and they were getting worse."

Torie felt a cold sweat break out along her spine. She could hear the blood rush to her temples as she experienced a slight tingle of adrenaline. "Are you talking about Effie and Hattie?"

Tilda nodded. "Yes, how do you know them?"

"Well, when the police were investigating your cousin's death, they found his mother. Bound to her bed. She was bound with black magic, and not in the best shape when we found her."

Tilda looked confused, shaking her head as her thoughts swirled. "That's not…it doesn't sound right. Are you sure?"

"We were there, Tilda. We saw what had been done to her," said Jasmin.

"What about my mother? I mean if Effie was bound with magic, my mother would have tried to free her. What did she say about that?"

Now it was Torie's turn to be confused. "Your mother wasn't there. She was in Oregon. She only just arrived and has been red noted with Effie. Terry, the mayor, refused to let Effie see or have contact with her sister for years."

Tilda looked wide-eyed and then began to laugh nervously.

"Lady, I don't know who you're talking about, but my mother lives with Effie in that house. I am the one that lived in Oregon and just flew out. What are you talking about?"

The chill that Torie had felt in her spine suddenly turned to an iceberg that made its way into her throat.

Jasmin cleared her throat and spoke up. "Where does your cousin live?"

"He lives, or rather, lived, at that house as well. He was afraid to leave the two of them alone and would never leave the house unless it was to go to work. Other than that, he never stepped a foot outside the house. Until recently."

"What happened recently?" asked Jasmin.

"He started texting me, said our parents had somehow tapped his phone and that they had gone too far with everything. He sent me pictures of...disgusting things, that he said they were collecting. He said they had finally figured it out."

"Were the things they collected in small, gilded boxes?" questioned Torie, her voice beginning to shake.

"Yes. Those...body parts." Tilda shivered and threw her arms around herself.

"Tilda, listen to me," said Jasmin. "What did they figure out how to do?"

Tilda took a deep breath. "They have always been jealous of the supernaturals in the community; especially the witches. They coveted their power and were determined to find a way to make it their own. They collected all kinds of spell books and tomes on magic, but other than a few fancy parlor tricks—like what I just tried against you— nothing worked.

"It consumed them, this hunt for powers. At first, we

thought it was all fine. They told us they wanted to become witches themselves so they could stop the real witches from terrorizing children. So we bought into it. But then, we started noticing little things. The cruelty they exhibited. The tired, southern racist tropes, and their disregard for what was right and wrong when it came to their single-minded pursuit of what they wanted.

"Terry overheard them talking about something one night, many years ago, that freaked him out so bad that he made me move across the country, far away from them. He wouldn't tell me what it was, just that for my own safety I needed to go. They were furious of course, and I lost contact with them, even with Terry, until recently when he reached out.

"He said they had been collecting those body parts or whatever, to appease some dark power. In return, that darkness was granting them magical abilities. But the magic was only allowing them to move through realms to get to where they could find the...donors they called them, for the sacrifices."

"Elion was right," said Jasmin. "Sacrifices to old gods probably in return for favors."

"Terry was terrified of what they were doing. He wanted to reach out to you two for help, but...honestly, we still weren't sure what you were or what you might do. He sent me instructions on something he needed me to do, and I flew in the day he stopped returning my calls to help him. I followed his directions and delivered the package to you. Then I came here and haven't left since. I wasn't sure what to do when Terry lost contact with me."

"What did you deliver?" Torie asked.

"A little cat," she said. "Terry said it was a very special

cat, but I just thought it was a weird-colored kitty. I left it in a basket on your porch and then hightailed it out of there."

Torie released a deep breath and stared at Jasmin. The implications of what Tilda had told them made her dizzy.

"Where did Terry get the cat?" asked Jasmin.

"Our parents had it at the house. It was going to be one of the sacrifices apparently. Although I don't know why. Terry said they had already taken the heart out of the cat's mother, so I don't know why they would need another one. But he sneaked it out of the house one day; hid it in a warehouse we used to play in when we were kids. That's where I picked it up.

"He was allergic to cats, you know. But this one must have been one of those breeds made for people with allergies. It seemed nice, but he texted me to be careful handling it because it bit him or scratched him or something, the morning he took it away from the house."

Again, the witches exchanged looks as Elion's warning about some dragons being poisonous came flooding back to them.

"Was the bite to his hand?" asked Torie.

Tilda nodded. "I think so. Why?"

Jasmin plopped herself down on the lower bunk opposite Torie.

"They played us," she said. "Those two crazy old bats played us this whole time."

Torie looked up at Jasmin, her eyes wide in fear.

"Jasmin, what have I let into my house?"

Chapter Twenty-One

Jasmin kept her foot pressed hard against the accelerator, screeching around curves and opening up on straight ways as they hurried back.

"Okay, I appreciate the urgency as much as anyone, but we won't do them any good if we die in a ditch before we get there," said Torie, grasping the handle above her door for dear life.

"Yeah," said Tilda from the back seat. "And why are you driving? Don't you have brooms?"

"Don't be ridiculous," said Torie. "We don't fly around on brooms." Then she lowered her voice and whispered to Jasmin. "Do we?"

The annoyed look that Jasmin gave her made her regret asking the question.

Jasmin was shaking her head and mumbling to herself.

"What's that?" asked Torie, even though the last thing she wanted was to distract Jasmin's attention as they hurtled down the road.

"I was just saying how could I be so stupid? Something

just didn't feel right, and I couldn't put my finger on it. Think about it. That shadow thing we saw at the mayor's house when we went back."

"You think that was Hattie?" asked Torie.

"Or some form of her."

"But why would she just let us take those boxes out of there? Those were obviously very important to them."

"No idea. At least not yet. We'll ask them when we get back."

"Assuming they talk," said Torie.

Jasmin looked over at her friend, a glint in her eyes. "Oh, them bitches will talk alright. We'll make sure of it."

"They may not be witches, but they have to have some kind of power we don't know about. How else would they have been able to take out a...mother cat...like that?"

Jasmin shook her head. "Don't know. Like Elion said, there isn't a lot known about those cats. We will add that to the list of questions."

They arrived at the house and Jasmin killed the lights and pulled off the main road just outside of her own house. Whatever was going on inside Torie's home, they didn't want to announce their presence just yet.

"What's the plan?" asked Torie as they stood at the top of the street looking down towards her house.

"We go in there *Lethal Weapon* style. Take them old biddies out before they know what hit them."

"Um, what about me?" asked Tilda.

"You stay here," said Torie. She wasn't entirely onboard with the idea of bringing her, but until they knew exactly what they were up against, she could also see the rationale of not leaving her unprotected at a campground.

"I wish we knew what was going on in there," said

Jasmin. "At least where everyone was. It seems awful quiet for a house full of supernaturals."

Torie jumped as a thought came to her. "I have an idea. Let me try something."

She closed her eyes and focused her mind on a single thought. "Leo," she whispered.

She felt a sense of vertigo as her conscious telescoped through the foliage towards her house and blasted through the walls. Everything was blurry and out of focus as she looked around, but she realized she was in her bedroom. The fact that her vision was centered mere inches from the floor was highly disconcerting.

She was seeing through Leo's eyes. The dragon was lying under her bed peering out.

Torie could sense the dragon's confusion and immediately sought to calm him. He recognized the touch of her mind, and she felt him start to grow at ease.

"Hi, buddy...I need to know what's going on in the house. Can you go downstairs and show me?"

The vertigo returned as her vision began to move, sliding across the floor and out of the room. The sensation of being right at floor level was something Torie hoped she would never have to get used to. When the dragon reached the stairs and bounded down them, she felt her stomach enter her throat a couple of times. Still, he made his way downstairs and crept along one wall towards the study.

Peering around the corner, Torie could see Effie and Hattie standing in the middle of the room holding one of the boxes.

She tried to hear what they were saying, but suddenly her ears were filled with heat and the sound of rushing water. She felt unbridled anger swelling in her breast as her lungs grew hot and liquid fire filled her throat.

Leo was about to fill the room with liquid lava.

Torie asserted her will as powerfully as she could, telling the dragon to stop. She felt resistance, but then, slowly, the rage began to recede. Recede, but not disappear. It felt like it had been locked behind a door and was tapping constantly to be let out.

"Not yet, little one. Where are my friends?"

Through emerald eyes, she looked around, and on the wall to the right of the sisters she saw Fionna, her mouth gagged with a handkerchief, her feet and hands bound. She lay on her side, not struggling to move. There was a gash on her forehead, and Torie had to fight the urge to have Leo run up to her so she could be close to her friend.

Just then, Fionna's eyes opened, and she saw Leo staring at her. She stared hard for a moment and then nodded slightly at him. Somehow, she knew that Torie was there with them. She looked determinedly at the sisters then back at Leo. Then, her vision focused on something in front of the sisters that Torie could not see.

Inching along the wall, she saw Elric, simply bound as Fionna, and she could tell the werewolf was unconscious. In front of the witches, Max was on his knees, his head moving slowly from side to side. His languid movements made it obvious he had been drugged.

Effie turned suddenly and looked at Leo. Torie was shocked at the change in the woman. She was still old, but her body had changed even more since Torie had last seen her. She was no longer stooped over but stood upright and sure of herself. The pallor of her skin had gone from translucent white to a healthier shade, and her movements were whip-sharp. Her milky eyes were still unseeing, but her hearing had obviously improved as well. Her head was cocked to one side as she focused on Leo.

Hattie turned to see what had caught her sister's attention, looked at Leo, and waved dismissively at him as they returned to what they were doing.

He still appeared as a cat to anyone other than supernaturals.

Torie willed Leo to leave the room and return to the safety of her bedroom and his hiding spot under the bed. As he turned and left the room, she returned to her body and focused on Jasmin.

"Those two sisters are in the study. I couldn't make out what they are doing, but they have got Elric and Fionna tied up. They're about to do something to Max. We need to get in there."

"What about Elion?" asked Jasmin.

Torie shook her head. "I didn't see him. Maybe in light of things, storming in may not be the best idea. They're more prepared than we thought. They somehow got the jump on three shifters. And who knows what they did to Elion."

"What if we went around back and came in through the kitchen? It's far enough from the study that they shouldn't hear anything."

"Worth a try," said Torie. "Plus, I always forget to lock those doors."

"You know I'm telling Elric that."

Torie ignored her as they made their way to one of the walking trails that ran along her property and followed it to the back of her lot. Once there, they were faced with the looming retention wall and the high iron bars meant to deter anyone from trying what they were about to try.

"Well, now I wish we had some broomsticks," Torie said, looking up.

"Take my hands," Jasmin said, holding both arms out.

Torie took them and watched as Jasmin closed her eyes.

> *"Spirits of light, hear my plea,*
> *make our bodies as mist, to go where we need."*

Instantly the ground faded away from beneath them and the air around them shimmered and passed through the two witches as their physical bodies grew ephemeral; losing all form and becoming gray smoke. Unencumbered by gravity, they floated upward, passing through the bars of Torie's fence like ghosts, only to settle on the patio beyond and reform into their physical selves.

Torie's hand went to her head as a rush of lightheadedness struck her.

"Easy there," said Jasmin, steadying her by gripping her arm. "The first time someone does that is always a doozie."

"I...had no idea that was a thing we could do," said Torie.

"Well, it's not something we want to make a habit of; it pretty much wipes me out for a bit. But come on, we can't stay out here."

As quietly as possible, Torie opened the patio door enough for them to slip through. Once in the kitchen, Torie noticed three coffee cups sitting on the island. They were half filled with coffee, and if she had to bet, that was how they were rendered unconscious. She doubted that the two women, or whatever they were, would have been able to get the drop on three shifters any other way.

Torie felt a flutter in her mind and knew that Leo had sensed her in the house. She mentally commanded him to remain where he was so as to remain safe and smiled to herself when she felt him settle back down.

Both she and Jasmin called up their magic, holding it at

the ready to strike out with if needed. As they crossed through the living room to head towards the study, Jasmin stopped to pick up an iron fire poker from beside the fireplace.

"Iron," she whispered. "It helps disrupt black magic. Hopefully, that's all we'll be dealing with."

"Good to know," said Torie, arming herself with the ash shovel.

Together the two witches crept down the hall, eyes on the light that shone from the doorway to the study.

"Why is it so quiet?" asked Torie. "I don't hear anything."

"Boo!" came a voice from behind them.

Jasmin spun just as Hattie swung a large stone from Torie's patio. She struck Jasmin in the head with a sickening crunch, dropping the witch where she stood.

Torie immediately raised her hands, blue fire swirling about them.

"Oh, I wouldn't," said Hattie, a dark grin splitting her face. "You might get me, but I'm betting Effie can end at least one of your friends before you can get in there. Hmm, now I wonder which one she will go after first?"

Torie dropped her magic and her hands, looking from the old woman to her best friend lying at her feet. Jasmin was so still that Torie couldn't tell if she was even breathing. The thought turned fear to barely contained rage, and she wanted nothing more than to blast this grinning woman into oblivion. But she also knew Hattie was right. No way she could take them both out in separate rooms.

"What do you want?" demanded Torie.

"Just to finish what we started. You'll see," said Hattie. "But first, put these on."

She tossed a pair of handcuffs in Torie's direction and watched as the witch slipped them onto her wrists.

"They're coated with a dead man's blood and an enchantment that should hold you long enough," said Hattie.

She was right. Torie felt weak as soon as she locked them in place. Her magic was still there, but it had faded far into the recesses of her being, just out of touch. She looked down again at Jasmin's still form.

"Leave her there," said Hattie. "Come on in. We've been waiting for you."

Torie walked ahead of her and entered the study. Effie was sitting on the chair at the far end of the room. In one hand, she held a fistful of Fionna's hair, holding the still-groggy shifter's head upright. In the other, she held a large butcher knife, the blade at Fionna's throat.

Her unfocused, gray eyes searched in Torie's direction, and she smiled.

"Well, well, well. Looks like the gang's all here."

"What do you want?" seethed Torie, trying to sound braver than she felt.

"What do I want?" repeated Effie. "I want your powers. But first, I want my eyes back."

Chapter Twenty-Two

"Now, sister," said Hattie, entering the room. She dropped the blood-stained rock on the floor with a thud. "You're going to get your eye. And soon we'll have more power than these witches could have ever dreamed of."

"If it's something you want from me, then let my friends go. I won't go anywhere. You have my word."

"Oh no, witch, there is nothing we need from you," said Hattie. "We have everything we need. Well, almost everything." She glanced over at Max who was slumped on the floor.

"What did you do to them?" asked Torie.

"A special strain of wolfsbane," the old woman replied. "It's deadly to them, you know. I laced their coffee with it. Not quite enough to kill them; just keep them docile long enough." She laughed and looked over at her sister. "And you thought their sense of smell would warn them. I told you it would work. This strain is undetectable. Now your friend there, the squirrel girl, she got the same sedative your friend Jasmin got. Sometimes, brute force works best."

"What took you so long to get back?" asked Effie. "I was thinking we were going to have to do this without you."

"You were expecting us?"

"Of course. As a matter of fact, I watched the two of you sneaking around back on your security system here. Sweet setup." Hattie nodded in the direction of the camera monitor on Torie's desk. "And sweet spell you used to get through the fence; I'm definitely going to add that one to our request."

Torie had no idea what she was talking about, but before she could say anything, Max groaned and began to move around on the floor.

"Oh no, we can't have that," said Hattie. She moved faster than Torie would have given a woman her age credit for. Scooping up a canvas bag off the desk chair, she reached in and took out a handful of black powder. Moving to stand next to Max and Elric, she threw it into the air, scattering it in their direction.

Instantly, Max dropped back to the floor, unconscious.

"Where's Elion?" asked Torie, looking around the room.

Hattie's eyes grew dark and hard. "Oh, that one. He was entirely too dangerous to fool with. We weren't taking any chances, so we bound him in the same black chains that I placed around Effie to fool you. And then, we sat him outside in the sun to roast for a bit. I doubt it will kill him, but who knows...maybe." She laughed again. "You and your friend walked right by him. He was bound to the far side of the fencing. Too weak to even call out to you. And you were so focused on getting in here that you never noticed him."

Torie's mind was racing. She remembered just how tough Elion was and she had to believe that he could survive whatever these two had thrown at him. Still, she feigned hurt at the woman's words, hoping it might goad her into talking even more.

"Oh, does it hurt you knowing that you weren't able to help such a disgusting creature like that? You should be ashamed of yourself, keeping company with these animals. Still—" she looked at Max, "—at least they will be put to good use."

"Why are you doing this?" Torie needed time to think. And the fact that this woman was in love with her own voice might just give her the time she needed to think of something. "And why here? Why my house?"

"Wouldn't you just like to know?" taunted Effie. "Don't tell her anything, Hattie."

"Be quiet," said Hattie, her tone forceful and tinged with warning. "I don't care if she knows; she can't do anything to stop it at this point." She faced Torie with a hateful sneer on her face. "We needed this house because it is steeped in lore. Like most witches, the first thing you do when moving into a place is erect wards and spells all around it. Magic that seeps into every nook and cranny. Well, what we are doing requires a space that has been mystically sanctified to work. Our old house just wouldn't cut it for the final big bang."

Torie closed her eyes, pretending to shake her head in horror at the witch's words. She was concentrating, reaching out to her unconscious friend in the hallway, probing at the recesses of her mind, imploring her to wake up.

"Jasmin, please. Wake up. We need you."

Unabated, the elderly woman continued, this time moving around to stand behind Max.

"You're not witches," said Torie quickly, drawing attention away from the unconscious werewolf.

"Oh, that's the beauty of sacrifices, dear; we don't have to be."

"It never works out. Whoever you are sacrificing to will want something in return. Something you probably won't be able to pay."

Hattie threw back her head in laughter. "We made a trade that the powers that be had not seen before."

She focused her eyes, and Torie watched in horror as they grew large and black; shiny, dark orbs that seemed impossibly big for her face. Her body shimmered then, seeming to go in and out of focus. One minute it was there, the next it became hazy and black, more shadow than physical form, and Torie recognized it from the brief glimpse she had at the mayor's house. But this time, the shadow was solid, and it maintained its grip on Max. Torie made a mental note; if it was solid, maybe she could hurt the creature.

"What have you done?" Torie said.

The shadowy figure that was Hattie laughed, the voice deep and scratchy.

"We offered our physical bodies up to the demons in exchange for the power of magic. We will be as powerful as you are, but without the limitation of the physical body. And in order to make that deal, all we had to give them were certain organs from some of those disgusting animal creatures." She waved her hand at the open boxes that were arranged on Torie's desk. "We were nearly complete, with the exception of the last, most important one they requested."

"You murdered shifters; and for what? To use their organs, along with your own bodies, as money to purchase some magical abilities. What is wrong with you?" spat Torie.

"Oh, not just shifters. We had a couple of humans in

the mix as well. Certain ones that they pointed out to us, and of course the dragon heart. That one was tricky, but they showed us a spell to make an old one shift into human form. After that, she didn't put up much of a fight.

"The last piece was the eye of an alpha supernatural. The dragon had a wee baby and we figured that would work. But that damned son of Effie's stole it away before we could complete the sacrifice. But luckily, this mutt is an alpha, with two eyes; one for the sacrifice and one for my sister."

"Mama, what are you doing?"

Tilda had come into the room, holding one side of the wall for support. Her face a mask of horror and disgust as she looked around the room.

"Tilda? What are you doing here? I should have known you'd be skulking around. Were you working with Terry? Where is our dragon pet?"

"I...I have no idea what you're talking about. But please...stop this, whatever it is you're doing."

Hattie waved an arm and Tilda was tossed through the air to crash in a heap on the floor.

It distracted the old women just enough for Torie to focus on the knife Effie held to Fionna's throat.

"Knife," she said, pulling the blade to her hand and away from Effie. It would do no good getting the cuffs off her, but it also wasn't pressed against Fionna's neck anymore. Just in time, because the squirrel shifter was conscious now, and in the blink of an eye shifted into her squirrel form, scampered behind Effie before shifting back to her human form, arm crooked around the old woman's neck.

"Step away from Max or I swear I will snap her neck," Fionna said.

"You will do nothing of the sort," said Effie. "Get your pervert hands off me!"

The old woman moved with unnatural speed and strength, driving her body backwards to slam Fionna into the wall, knocking the breath out of her as she slid down onto her bottom. Effie's own figure began to shimmer as she took on a similar look as her sister. This time, her hand elongated, fingers stiffening with razor-sharp, black talons that erupted through the skin. She drove her hand in the direction of Fionna's head with enough force to penetrate her skull.

But the killing blow never connected as her hand stopped in midair, trapped in a bubble of blue magic.

Torie turned to see Jasmin braced against the doorjamb, holding herself up with one arm as she extended the other, her hex power crackling around her. Blood poured from the gash on her head, mixing with sweat as the exertion of using power was taking its toll on her injured body.

With one final heave, Jasmin threw her arm back, using the power that encircled Effie's hand to fling the old woman across the room to crash at her sister's feet. The effort proved too much for her, and Jasmin dropped to the floor, unconscious. Tilda ran over to her, bending down to attend the witch in any way she could.

Hattie laughed as Effie scampered to her feet, unharmed by the attack.

"Time to finish this and get our final reward," said Hattie.

With that, she grabbed the unconscious form of Max and held him up.

Effie stood over him and spoke.

"In darkness' name I offer you this,

a gift from a body that twists and shifts.
Take these gifts and build anew,
a body that is equal among the few."

With that, she watched as Effie drove her long, pointed fingers into Max's eye, pulling it free and throwing it into the one empty box. The shock roused Max out of his stupor, and the wolf howled with pain, grabbing at his mangled eye as he writhed on the floor.

As soon as the eye hit the box, all of them erupted in a blast of light and smoke as the organs disintegrated in a blinding flash.

Torie was mortified and screamed in horror at the carnage. She channeled her anger into action, calling on her hex power. The knife she held in her hand glowed white-hot as she sent it screaming at the women. It struck Hattie, burying itself hilt-deep into the woman's shoulder.

Torie's eyes glowed with power as she felt a click behind her back and the handcuffs dropped off her wrists. She looked over to see Tilda cradling Jasmin's head in her lap. The witch was awake but barely able to focus her eyes. She held one finger aloft, having summoned enough power to set Torie free.

Torie raced across the room reaching to grab the knife from Hattie's shoulder to use as a weapon, only to find herself in Effie's steely grip as the old demon held her from behind.

"We really were going to let you live, you know?" said Effie, her breath hot and fetid against Torie's cheek.

"I opened my home to you, and this is what I get in return," said Torie. "You are a terrible houseguest. Luckily you aren't my only one."

"What?" said Effie, just as Hattie pulled the knife out of

her arm and moved to stand by her sister, her face ablaze with anger and hate.

Torie looked down in front of her, and Hattie's eyes followed.

"What is it? What do you see, sister?" demanded Effie.

"It's just her damned cat. It can watch as we finish her." Torie laughed and spoke.

"Lady of Light heed my call,
and let that which is hidden be seen by all."

At the same time, she lifted her leg and stamped down on Effie's instep, while driving the back of her head into the demon's nose, causing her to release her grip. Torie spun, facing Effie and drove the side of her hand into Effie's throat. The old woman gasped, grabbing at her neck in pain just as Torie threw herself to the side, away from the two women.

She watched, seeing the look of shock and recognition on Hattie's face as she saw Leo for what he truly was.

Leo drew himself up onto his hind legs, his little wings flapping furiously as he rose into the air until he hovered a foot above the two old women. His eyes gleamed as he drew in a deep breath and exhaled, belching lava-hot fire at the two of them.

Torie shielded her eyes from the brightness as the conflagration engulfed the two screaming women, turning skin and bone to ash.

Once done, the little dragon settled onto the floor next to Torie, licking lightly at her bruised form.

"It's okay, I'm alright," she said.

She clamored to her feet and moved over towards Jasmin to check on her friend.

"I'm okay," Jasmin said, waving her off. "Go check on Max."

Torie limped over to the still writhing werewolf and tried to console him. She held his head and placed a hand over his eye, pouring forth warmth and magic. When it did nothing, she turned her magic to a more calming effect that acted as a pain killer, sedating him long enough for her to get to Fionna.

Fishing her phone out of her pocket, she dialed a couple of numbers, spoke quickly and headed back to where Jasmin and Tilda were sitting on the floor.

"Glen's on her way with some help. Just hold on."

She watched as her best friend tried to smile, before closing her eyes once again.

"So other than Max, everyone is going to be fine," Glen said, as she dabbed some antibiotic ointment onto the gash on Jasmin's head. "But you're going to have to take it easy for a few days. Nothing strenuous at all, deal?"

Jasmin nodded, looking over at her friends. Torie, Fionna and Elric were attending to Max. The big wolf sat on the arm of a couch as one of Glen's trusted co-workers took one more set of vitals on the Sheriff. There was a white bandage around his head securing a gauze pad over his ruined eye.

"Will it grow back?" asked Jasmin, nodding in his direction.

"No idea," said Glen. "From what I know, shifters, wolves in particular, have amazing regenerative abilities. But this was a bad one, so he may well be maimed for life."

Jasmin looked over at Elion, who was seated alone in the room. She got up and walked carefully over to him.

"You okay?" she asked.

The vampire nodded. "I will be."

His skin was dark and sloughing off in places, deep blisters and pustules had formed on his cheeks and chest where he had suffered direct exposure to the sunlight.

"Elion, this should have killed you. I've never heard of a vampire surviving this kind of exposure to sunlight."

"Well, it's a good thing I'm not like most vampires then, isn't it?"

Jasmin didn't say anything as Torie walked over to them and gave her friend a gentle hug.

"So, I know you wanted to have a memorable house-warming party, but that was just a little over the top," said Jasmin. "I am so glad that is over."

Torie sighed deeply. "I *hope* it's over."

"What do you mean?" asked Jasmin.

"I'm still trying to figure out just what Hattie and Effie did. Sure, they gave their bodies up for possession, but... there was something else. Something about the last part of that incantation. She said something about creating a body that was equal among the few; one that was built anew. What did that mean?"

Jasmin shook her head. "Who knows? Right now, I'm just glad they are both gone, thanks to little Leo there." She looked over at the dragon, who seemed content to curl up under the desk and nap throughout the commotion. "Whatever comes next, we will deal with that too. But for now, let's enjoy this small victory that we made it through unscathed. Well, most of us anyway." Her eyes softened as they settled on Max, who was thanking the paramedic for his help and assuring him he needed no more care.

"You know, one other thing bothers me too. Who cast a glimmer spell on Leo to make him look like a cat to humans? There has to be more to this than we know."

"I guess we'll figure that out when the time comes as well. But for now, I guess this means you're keeping the dragon."

Torie smiled. "He's part of the family now. He saved our lives, so yeah…he can stay as long as he wants."

Jasmin smiled. "I guess family comes in all shapes and forms in these parts. Literally."

They laughed and made their way over to the rest of their friends, thankful, hopeful that time would heal all wounds.

Chapter Twenty-Three

Torie made her way through the mass of people in her house, swerving and spinning to keep from bumping into her laughing and chatting guests. She was nervous about there not being enough food or drink for the housewarming, despite having made enough food to feed a veritable army.

She made her way between guests to the kitchen to check on the makeshift bar she had set up, along with multiple charcuterie boards along the massive center island. The wine was definitely getting low, so she took out a few more bottles of white and rose to stick into the silver ice bins. She opened a few more bottles of red and placed them strategically around the boards. Luckily the waiters she had hired to assist had been keeping the boards filled with cuts of Italian ham and pepperoni, as well as fruits and cheeses of all kinds.

Along the outer wall of the kitchen was a large banquet table covered from end to end with chocolate confections of all kinds. Everyone who would have normally taken part in the chocolate contest at the festival had been asked to bring their creation to her house for everyone to enjoy. She smiled, surveying all the homemade goodies that added an incredible aroma that permeated the entire house.

Frederica Morris was circling the island from the far side, a small plate of cheese and grapes in one hand as she surveyed the details and appliances of the custom kitchen. Torie smiled at the realtor and made her way over to her.

"Hello, Frederica, how are you doing today?" She had wanted to check in on the woman to see how she was doing after the harrowing experience of finding the mayor's mother and thinking the woman dead.

"Torie! I'm doing just fine, all things considered. It's not every day you find a body that turns out to not be a body. Can you imagine?"

She actually could but rather than say that, she just shook her head and made a small clucking sound in commiseration.

"I mean, when I tell you that woman looked dead, she looked *dead*. But then, I guess I must have blacked out after that, because I don't remember anything after seeing her," she continued.

"Well, it is probably for the best."

"And the weird thing is, no one seems to know what happened to that poor woman's body. It's like she just disappeared." Her voice trailed off, and Torie could tell her mind was trying to pick at the broken memories of the event.

"So, what do you think of the house? I'm happy with the way it turned out."

Immediately the realtor snapped out of her reverie and her face lit up.

"Oh, Torie, it is immaculate. I mean, personally I would have gone with a more traditional, neutral color scheme, especially in the kitchen; but you do you, as they say. Now, if you ever decide that this big old house is too much for you, I will be more than happy to get you top dollar for it."

Torie smiled. "Thank you, but I think this is going to be home for me."

She excused herself and made her way out of the kitchen where she bumped into Tilda.

"Tilda, how's it going? I'm glad you decided to stay around a bit."

Tilda reached out to shake her hand. "Thank you. And thank you for everything. I still feel awful knowing what my mom and my aunt put you and your friends through."

"Don't even think about it. If there is one thing I've learned since moving here, it's that you can't choose your family. But you can make one."

Tilda smiled, nodding.

"So, what are you thinking about doing? Heading out west again, or…?"

"I've been thinking about that. Honestly, I think I'm going to stay here for a while. I've even thought about running for mayor, taking over the work my cousin was doing."

Torie's eyes grew wide. "That would be amazing. You can certainly stay here until you figure out what you need to do. And when you're ready, I know a realtor that I'm betting will be more than happy to help you find a house."

She gave Tilda's arm a squeeze and then moved on, looking for Jasmin.

She found her, standing alone in the corner of the great room watching the other guests and sipping from a whiskey glass. There was a rolling bar cart in the room and Torie poured herself a shot of bourbon and joined her.

"Cheers," she said with a smile as they clinked their

glasses together. "Are you sure you should be drinking? You have a concussion."

"*Had* a concussion. I'm feeling much, much better. Besides, I was going stir-crazy lying in bed, and you know I was not about to miss this. It was a great idea you had, having this drop-in. I've seen so many folks from town that never go to social functions. Goes to show that everyone knows your name and they respect you."

Torie smiled at her friend. "Honestly, I just thought it would be a good way to get to know everyone and for them to get to know us. I just keep thinking about the way that Tilda and the mayor were raised to fear and hate witches. It was almost indoctrination. Plus, Hattie and Effie weren't much better in their thoughts of us. Jealousy consumed them and led them to make a literal deal with demons. If I am truly going to be a part of this community, I want people to know the real me. Same goes for you and Fionna, and every other supernatural member of this town. I mean, that is if you want that as well."

Jasmin leaned her head on her friend's shoulder. "I'm all good with all of that. I mean, we can't go hanging a sign outside of our houses that says, 'Witch Lives Here', but we need to start slowly adjusting the narrative in Singing Falls. Letting people know that they are safe here. I believe they already feel that way, thanks in large part to you." She motioned with her glass towards Fionna, who was beaming as she made the rounds with Glen. "Look at her. She's in her glory." Jasmin had found a sash that said, 'Birthday Girl' and Fionna wore it with pride, basking in all the congratulations and well wishes.

"Oh, that reminds me," said Torie, clapping her hands together. "It's time for the last surprise of the evening."

She moved to the center of the room and held up her hands to speak.

"Everyone, if I could have your attention for a moment?" She paused as everyone slowly made their way into the great room, plates and drinks in hand. "First, thank you all for dropping by to say hello and be part of this housewarming-slash-birthday-party. It truly is my honor to have so many of you in my home. Second, I know that it was a blow to the town to have to cancel the Festival, but in light of the tragedy that befell our mayor, I can certainly understand the need to cancel it. But I have a feeling that the festival will be back next year, and larger than ever. In the meantime, feel free to enjoy all the wonderful chocolates that were made by many of the people in this very room.

"Now, to that end, I want to add my own contribution, in the form of the birthday cake in honor of one of my dearest friends. Fionna Goodridge, can you come up please?"

Smiling from ear to ear, Fionna moved to stand next to Torie.

"I want to say happy birthday to my dear friend, who means more to me than she knows. You, along with your beautiful wife, accepted me into this town and your heart, and for that I am eternally grateful. So, to mark the occasion of your first official birthday party, I made you something special."

The crowd parted as the waiters pushed in a large cart with a massive, four-tiered cake covered with beautiful orange and chocolate flowers growing in a spiral around it. An array of lit candles completed the display.

"It is a chocolate cake with a chocolate cream frosting. The chocolate flowers are called angel's trumpets and they are completely edible. I hope you enjoy it."

Fionna's eyes welled as she beheld the creation before her.

"I don't know what to say, other than thank you. Thank you everyone. You have no idea what this means to me."

She fought back her tears as she stood by the cake, closed her eyes, and then made a courageous attempt at blowing out the candles, laughing when she realized it would take a couple more breaths to get them all out.

Once the cake was sliced and being passed around, Torie slid next to Jasmin.

"Have you seen Elric lately?"

Jasmin looked around between bites of cake. "No, not since earlier. You guys have a fight? And, can I just say this is delicious! These angel's trumpet chocolates would have definitely taken first prize."

"Why thank you. I have you and your lovely green thumb to thank for the orange and chocolate inspiration. And no, we did not have a fight."

"He's probably with Max somewhere," she said as they walked out of the great room and into the kitchen. "Wolves of a feather and all that...oh there he is."

She pointed with her fork at the doors that led to the patio. Outside, on the far end of the patio, Elric was standing with Max and Elion. His arms flailed and his body was stiff as he jabbed animatedly at the air. Max was clearly trying to calm him down as Elion watched on. There was another figure standing with them; a woman that Torie did not recognize.

"Wonder what's going on out there." said Jasmin.

"I don't know, but I think we should go find out."

Together, they walked outside into the cool, evening air. Elion and Max were arguing over something, their voices low but tense.

"—you think will happen if we don't ask her for help?" Max was saying in a harsh whisper as Torie and Jasmin approached. When he saw them, he signaled for Elion to stop talking and the two of them acted as nonchalantly as possible.

"What's going on, guys?" asked Torie.

"Yeah, and what will happen if you don't ask who for help?" added Jasmin.

"It...it's nothing, really," said Max as he fidgeted with the black eyepatch, adjusting the strap that held it in place.

Torie looked at them, and then at the woman who stood next to Elric. She held one arm across her midsection, clasping the elbow of her other arm and would not take her eyes off the ground in front of her.

When no one said anything, Torie reached across the space in front of the two werewolves and held out a hand in introduction.

"Hello, I don't think we've met. I'm Torie, and this is my friend Jasmin."

"I'm Sable. It's nice to meet you."

She shook Torie's hand firmly, then stepped back, pushing a stray strand of her long, dark hair out of her face. She was tall, taller than both Jasmin and Torie. She wore fashionable jeans with a gray tank top tucked in that only accentuated her dancer's body. She wore minimal makeup and if Torie had to guess, she would put her age in her mid-thirties.

She gave Elric a look that caused her cheeks to redden before she broke eye contact and looked at Torie.

"Okay, so what's going on here, Elric?" Torie asked. She wanted to add *and why is this woman standing so close to you and giving you eyes like that*, but she didn't.

Elric took a deep breath and started to speak but then said nothing, preferring to look around at Max and Elion.

"Oh, for God's sake," said Sable, shaking her head. "There's just no easy way to say this so I'll just say it. I grew up with Elric." She took a deep breath before blurting out, "He's my fated mate."

Torie felt the air rush out of her lungs and looked to Jasmin for help, only to see the witch's mouth hanging open in surprise.

"Your...mate?" Torie said, suddenly needing to sit down.

"Yes, but it's not what you're thinking, Torie," said Elric, rushing forward to grasp her arm and steady her.

"No, it isn't," added Sable. "I don't...I don't want Elric. That's not why I'm here."

Torie's world was still reeling and she wasn't in the mood to play twenty questions.

"Then why are you here?"

"She is here because of me," said Elion. The vampire drew himself to his full height as he spoke his first words to them. "We are in love, Torie, and we need you to figure out a way to sever the link between two fated wolves."

"Because if you don't, our pack will come to find us; and they will tear everyone in this town apart," said Sable. "So, I'm begging you; can you break the bond that joins me to your boyfriend?"

vinci-books.com/moonlight

Magic, danger and destiny collide.

Torie, a witch in Singing Falls, must break a fated-mate bond between two werewolves, sparking a turf war and unleashing a deadly force. Can she protect her town before it's torn apart?

Turn the page for a free preview…

Moonlight Hexes: Chapter One

Torie Bliss sat on her patio, a soft, cashmere throw around her shoulders as she stared into the distance. Beyond the iron fence that wrapped her property, the large evergreens that heralded the entrance to the imposing forest of trees swayed slightly in the evening breeze. Every now and then, a sudden rustling of branches would reach her ears as squirrels leapt from one treetop to another. In the distance, owls hooted and called to one another as they organized themselves into hunting parties that frightened so many of the smaller woodland creatures that scampered about.

As the sun faded, the night air would blanket the North Carolina mountains, causing her to shiver just a little and draw her blanket tighter about her.

Something moved and stretched next to her, and she looked down to see Leo sitting on the comfortable cushion. The little dragon sensed her chill and hopped down, scampering to the fire pit that was situated not far from where Torie sat. He climbed onto the rim of the circular, stone pit, and blew orange fire down into it, causing the pit to flare to life, the tinder and logs inside bursting into flames.

Torie smiled, thankful for the warmth, and settled back, her thoughts far away as Leo climbed back onto the outdoor sofa and curled up in her lap.

She heard the back door open and close and looked over to see Elric walking towards her, carrying two glasses and a bottle of wine. He sat the bottle on the side table next to the sofa, poured the wine and handed one of the glasses to her before seating himself.

"Thank you," Torie said, lightly clinking her glass to his as he settled his body next to hers.

"I was going to ask if you wanted me to start a fire for you, but I see someone has already beat me to it."

Torie smiled, one hand stroking the dragon's back as he began to drift off to sleep in her lap.

"He has certainly come a long way," said Elric. "And it's obvious that he loves you."

Something in his voice made her look over at the werewolf, his eyes glinting in the crackling glow of the flames as he gazed out over the landscape.

Torie reached over and took one of his hands in hers. "I know how you feel about me. you don't have to project it onto a dragon, Elric."

"I know. It's just that, you've been so quiet lately. Ever since Sable came to town. I know you need time and distance, and I'm willing to give you both; I just don't want you to ever think how I feel about you has changed."

At the mention of the she-wolf that had shown up at her housewarming party, Torie felt the corners of her mouth drop, and she shifted her weight uncomfortably. It took her a moment to realize she was squeezing Elric's hand a little harder than was necessary, and she forced herself to relax her grip.

She sighed, dropping her head back to rest on the padded back of the sofa.

"I'm sorry if I've given you the impression that I feel that way. But you're right, I needed...I need...time to process."

She wanted to add, it's not every day the man you opened your heart to tells you he has a fated mate he was preordained to be with forever.

The look in Elric's eyes told her that she didn't have to say it aloud; the wolf was almost as good at reading her as the dragon was.

"We need to talk about this, Torie," he said, rubbing the top of her hand with his thumb. "We don't have a lot of time."

"I know. It's just a lot to take in. I guess what really bothers me is that you never told me about this. We've talked about everything over the last year. We've made plans, Elric. And it never occurred to you to tell me that you're...I don't even know what to call it."

"Fated. I am fated to be with another."

She withdrew her hand from his grasp. "I hate that word. Fated." It sounded so primitive to her ears. No, primitive wasn't right; it sounded *primal*.

They had spoken very little since the housewarming party; Torie had occupied herself with unpacking the last of her personal belongings and getting her new house in order, and Elric had given her the space he instinctively knew she needed. He had spent time working with Max, his old alpha leader who was now the sheriff of the tiny community of Singing Falls.

The town had been incredibly busy of late; new supernaturals and humans alike had moved into the picturesque town perched on the side of a mountain. The scenic beauty of the mountain provided them with temperate weather that consisted of warm days and cool nights, and mostly sheltered them from severe winter storms. It had attracted a lot of interest in individuals looking for someplace away from the big cities. A place that provided a sense of community and encouraged a live and let live attitude.

The fact that it was a haven for supernatural creatures who were tired of being hunted, either by their own kind or humans, had spread among shifter clans, and many had moved to Singing Falls looking for a new start. Some humans were aware of who and what they lived among; others might have sensed something different about certain townsfolk, but they didn't ask.

Live and let live was the unspoken motto.

Max, a werewolf like Elric, had taken on the role of the town sheriff and helped to protect the town's secret when it came to the outside world. Elric had recently taken a position as a forest ranger, patrolling the higher mountain hiking trails and lake communities that were experiencing a population boom at the moment. It was perfect for him in that it allowed him to spend time outdoors where he was at his most comfortable, while simultaneously letting him keep an eye out for anything unsavory that might come down from the silver areas to the north of Singing Falls or up into town from their more savage sister city, Trinity Cove.

It was part of his wolf nature to claim a territory, and consciously or not he had claimed Singing Falls. Not the least of which was because it's where the woman he loved resided.

Unfortunately, claiming a territory wasn't the only part of his werewolf heritage that had begun to show itself.

"It is something that was arranged long before I was the man I am today," he said to her.

They had never really talked much about it, but time was growing short, and Torie sensed the urgency that played into his words. She took a deep draw of her wine and turned to face him.

"So, this woman, Sable, do you love her?"

"No, not in the way that I love you." There was no hesitancy, and that made her feel a little better at least.

"So not like you do me, but does that mean you do have *some* kind of feelings for her?"

"I would be lying if I said I did not," the wolf replied, sipping from his own glass. "But it's more like a sense of protection I feel. It is familial love, not romantic. Until I met you, I did not know there was a difference. But I always suspected there had to be more to life than just what was involved in the packs."

"Why didn't you stay with her if that was the only life you knew?"

"Because I didn't even know her. We weren't from the same pack. As a matter of fact, we were from warring packs. Our union was the first time fated mates had been found outside of our immediate pack. We were unique, and the leaders of both packs thought our union would be a way to end our territorial fight. We would be united into a single, large pack and would spread our dominance over the entire Northeast region."

"You once told me you were born and raised in the upper territories of Maine, right?"

Elric nodded. "The northern reaches of Maine are very desolate. There aren't a lot of people living up there, and almost no towns to speak of. It is so remote that what roads there are do not have names.

"The pack that Max and I are from was one of the largest in the region. We held sway of the land east of the great lake that divided the range. The other pack, the Idle Winds pack, controlled the area to the west of the lake. Of course, each pack wanted what the other had, so there was constant fighting among them. It wasn't for me."

He stopped and drank more wine, reaching over to lazily pet Leo as he stretched in his sleep.

"At what age did you know you were fated to someone?" Torie asked.

"Age for werewolves is not the same as what it is for humans. Being a beta, I didn't even know it was possible to have a fated mate; typically, that is reserved for alphas."

"Like Max," Torie said.

Elric nodded. "Yes, the alphas are fated, but anyone below that on the social scale would typically just end up with whomever they hit it off with. Kind of like humans in that regard."

"Elric, what happened with Max then? Why isn't he with his mate?"

"She was killed in a brutal encounter with the Idle Winds pack. Things were getting heated between our packs, and one day, Max thought it would be a good idea to do some scouting in an area where our territories overlapped. It wasn't unheard of, that wolves can have certain spots that you would consider no-man's land. An area that any who were brave enough could enter.

"He had caught the scent of some game and was tracking it, along with Atema, his mate. They were ambushed. He escaped, but she...well, Max has never forgiven himself for that. I think that is part of the reason he was so willing to leave the pack with me and head south until we eventually came across Trinity Cove. And well, you know everything that has happened with us since then."

"You said that was part of the reason he left. What was the other?"

Elric took a deep breath and remained quiet for a moment. Torie stood and topped up their drinks, waiting for him to continue.

"It was around that time that I felt the call of my mate. I am not really sure how to explain it. It's like a scent on the breeze that you experience with all of your senses at once. It's a longing that pulls at you, and the more you ignore it, the harder it yanks. Until finally, you head off alone, into the woods, to find the source. That's what I did. Left my pack for a couple of days until I had hiked far into the ranges above the lakes.

"And that was when I met Sable. She had felt the pull as well. When two fated mates find one another, it can be quick, because you are both born into the same pack. But with us, we were pulled together far away from the eyes of our packs. I suppose it would have been fine had we settled down where we were, starting our own pack in an unmarked territory. But we decided not to do that. We were strangers to one another and were each wary of the other."

"So, did the two of you...?" Torie couldn't bring herself to finish the sentence.

"Mate? No, we did not. We resisted the urge, because we both knew that once we did that, the bond between us could only be separated by death."

His voice trailed off, and Torie could tell that something had registered on his supernatural senses. Leo lifted his head off her lap, his snout quivering in the flickering light as his body began to vibrate slightly.

"What is it?" she said to Elric.

Then she saw it; a shadow separated from the darkness of the trees and sprinted towards her property.

She stood quickly, calling up her magic to hold at the ready until Elric held out a hand, letting her know it was okay. In the blink of an eye, the shadow reached her retaining wall and, leaping high into the air, cleared it and the iron fence atop the rock wall, before casually walking up to the fire.

"Hello, Elion," said Elric. "You really should announce yourself better."

"Forgive me, but there was little time." He nodded to Torie and then turned to face Elric. "He has dispatched scouts, and I believe one of them picked up Sable's scent a few miles south of here."

Elric stiffened, causing a sudden spike in Torie's adrenaline.

"What are you talking about?" she said, "And who dispatched scouts?"

"You haven't told her?" said Elion.

"We were just getting to that part," replied Elric.

Torie looked at both supernaturals, arching her eyebrows in expectation. "Tell me what?"

Elric turned to her. "The big reason Max left the pack was because of the ruler of the Idle Winds pack. In retribution for the death of his fated one, Max killed the fated of their alpha. That alpha was his brother."

Moonlight Hexes: Chapter Two

Torie was shocked at the revelation and didn't know what to say. She stared hard at Elric, who could only swallow hard, taking a long drink from his glass.

"Were you a part of that?" asked Torie.

"No. I did not know what he had done until it was too late. After that, there was nothing more Max could do. He had to run. Staying with the pack would have meant all-out war, and as we were no match for the size of his brother's pack, it would have meant certain death for everyone.

"By running, it removed the need for confrontation. I, being Max's second, left with him. That created a second problem. It meant Sable had no fated mate. No one knew I was to be her mate, so Max's brother chose her to become his new mate. He lied about there being a fated bond between them and forced her to be his. I assume she ran as well at some point. We ended up in Trinity Cove, and apparently, so did Sable." He looked at Elion, and the vampire could only nod.

"She was drawn to Trinity Cove because you were

214

here," Elion said. "She tried to blend in with the community over the past year. Even once you were gone, she felt like she had found a place where she could start over again, far from the watchful eyes of a demanding pack."

"So what, then the two of you met and fell in love?" asked Torie.

"Yes," Elion said matter-of-factly. "That is exactly what happened."

"And you had no idea she was here?" Torie turned to Elric.

"No. I had already established myself here by the time she arrived. We only found out when I met up with Elion to help us with Leo. He told Max and I that Sable was in town, and that they had become involved."

"Is that why you stayed here?" asked Torie. "Is that what you wanted all along? Someone to break the fated bond between Elric and Sable?"

Elion nodded, though he could not meet Torie's gaze.

"We don't even know if it is possible," he said. "The few witches we knew back in Trinity Cove would not attempt it; they had no interest in involving themselves in something that could be considered an act of war with a large pack of werewolves."

"So then, what makes you think I would try it?"

Elion looked from her to Elric and back again. "Because you have as vested an interest in this as I do. As long as Elric is bonded to Sable, then neither of them is completely free of the other."

Torie didn't say anything, her heart racing and her mind swirling with thoughts. She didn't know how to feel. She picked up her glass and slowly walked to the edge of the deck, looking out. Elric moved to stand beside her and placed a tentative hand on her shoulder. He felt her body tense in response and let it drop to his side.

"Elion, can you give us some space please?" Elric said.

The vampire hesitated, then nodded. "Of course." He disappeared into the house, leaving them alone in the flickering light of the fire.

Silence, punctuated by the far-off sound of frogs and the occasional hoot of an owl, seemed more pervasive than the darkness that had crept across the grounds before them.

"Why didn't you tell me, Elric?"

The big wolf sighed. "Because I didn't want to think about it. By the time I realized the true depth of my feelings for you, I thought it was too late."

"No, that was exactly when you should have told me."

"I didn't know what it meant myself. I thought that with distance and time, the bond would fade. I'm no alpha; I didn't have the right to a fated mate. I thought it couldn't be true, that maybe I had somehow misread the signs."

Torie spun to face him, her face wet as she fought back tears. "And what about Sable? Do you think she felt the same way? Why did she follow you here if she didn't feel something?"

"I don't know, Torie. I can't tell you what's in her mind or why she fled the pack. I can only tell you what I felt. And what I didn't feel." He reached out and gently wiped at her tears with his thumb. "What I didn't feel was love. Deep down, I knew that no matter what, I would never feel for Sable the way you're supposed to feel for the one you love with all your heart and soul. I think I knew that I was destined for someone else." He leaned in and kissed her on the forehead, his lips lingering. "But now I do. And I am terrified of losing that."

Torie took his hand in hers and kissed it.

"I never meant to make you angry, Torie."

"I'm not angry. Just a little sad." *And that feels worse than anger right now.*

"So, what should we do?" he asked. "I am not going to have you do anything you are uncomfortable with. I made this mess. I'm fine taking my lumps and cleaning it up the hard way."

"What is the hard way?"

"Well, at some point, Arin will find Sable. And once he's in Trinity Cove, he will realize that Max and I are here as well. He'll see it as an opportunity to get revenge on Max, take out me, and unite the two Northeast packs under his one rule."

"I can see why he would be after Max, but why would he want to kill you? It's not like you even want to be with Sable."

"Because wolves mate for life. The only way to force Sable into a new fated mate bond would be to kill her existing mate."

"Christ. You think he would actually kill you over a misplaced love? Maybe even his own brother?"

Elric nodded. "There is a strong sense of family with wolves, but it is not the same as with human siblings. Both Max and Arin were born alphas. That's almost unheard of among werewolves. They fought constantly as children, until finally, their father kicked them both out of his pack and they were each forced to create their own. Each moved to a different side of the great lake and began to build their tribe. The result...well, you know what has happened since then.

"There is still a great animosity between them, and Arin knows this is his chance to take power. Whoever rose to take

Max's place in our old pack will not stand a chance against Arin."

"So why not just take that person out and take over the packs?"

"Because the true leader will always be Max. As long as he's alive, there is always a chance he could return and cause trouble for Arin. Plus, as long as Max lives, Arin will never have the complete, slavish loyalty that he craves from everyone around him. He has to kill Max to cement his place.

"And believe me. He will kill him, without hesitation."

"God, this is all so awful. I can't say that I understand any of it, but I'm not going to stand around and watch you get killed in some crazed, Shakespearean-werewolf drama."

"There is one other thing," Elric said, his voice low. "The wolves aren't the only problem we may have to contend with. The vampires undoubtedly know about Elion and Sable by now."

"So? What do they care?"

"The union of a werewolf and a vampire is considered unnatural. It's never happened before, and the vampires are not going to be happy about it."

"So, you're saying that if the bond between you and Sable isn't broken, it results in a lot of killing. If it is broken, and she and Elion can hook up, it results in a lot of killing? Great."

"This is all more than should have been dropped in your lap. This is my fault."

"No, it isn't, and don't think that way. But at least now I think I know why no other witches would take this on."

Elric nodded. "They know the history between were-wolves and vampires and were not willing to step into that."

Torie sensed there was more to that story, but she wasn't

ready to hear it. She was tired; the emotional rollercoaster she had just rode had worn her down. She needed rest and time to process.

"Come on, let's go to bed," she said. "We can call Jasmin tomorrow and talk this all through. Hey, I didn't ask, where is Sable staying?"

"She is at the Wandering Brook bed and breakfast in town."

Torie nodded. That was a good location. It was run by a fox shifter named Nora, and it wasn't far from the police station, so Max could help keep an eye on things as needed.

They walked through the kitchen, placing their wine glasses in the deep farmhouse sink, and found Elion sitting next to the fireplace in the great room.

"I'm going to talk to Jasmin tomorrow to see what we can do," said Torie.

The vampire looked up in surprise.

"I had expected you to say no. Not that I would blame you."

"Well, I'm not making any promises; so, don't get your hopes up. But I'll do what I can to help."

Torie had hoped the wine would help her sleep, but it had had the opposite effect on her. She lay there, alternating between staring at the ceiling and staring at the man she had come to love.

And he loved her. She knew that beyond a shadow of a doubt; but still, there was so much about the supernatural she didn't understand. What if having Sable this close to them could trigger something in Elric? Would he go back to her? Is the bond between fated mates stronger than human love?

She reached over and stroked his hair, smiling as he mumbled in his sleep and scooted his body closer to hers.

She felt tears building up. She had never felt anything like this before, and she knew that at this point in her life, she probably never would again.

This was something she wanted. Something she couldn't bear the thought of losing.

Something she wouldn't lose.

Maybe she couldn't break the bond between her beloved and the she-wolf, at least not without Jasmin's help, but maybe she could weaken it?

Her brow furrowed as she mulled that thought over in her head. Elric was obviously torn by what needed to be done, so this would be her way of offering him some solace in the matter. And she wouldn't tell him about it. It could be something she could do that would just live in the background, right?

No harm, no foul.

She thought for a moment and then closed her eyes, placing one hand lightly on Elric's forehead.

> *"By the powers of the moon, and blessed ides,*
> *let me be the only one, in this man's eyes.*
> *Let chains that were tight, now stretch thin,*
> *to grant free will to both wolves and men."*

She caught herself holding her breath as she watched for any signs that her spell had worked. But what exactly would happen? Finally, she let out a breath and realized there might be no way of knowing if the spell even worked. It had been a good thought, but obviously she was way out of her league with the kind of magic needed for this, so she curled up against Elric, pulled the covers around her, and feel into a deep sleep.

The next morning, Jasmin was sitting at the large kitchen island, a box of fresh scones sitting in front of her while the aroma of coffee filled the room.

"Absolutely not. No way," she said, her eyes narrowing at Torie, who blinked wide eyes at her.

"Well, don't you think it's something we should consider? Or at least talk about?"

"It sounds like it's something you've already considered. You're just looking for me to agree with you."

Torie realized she wasn't wrong. Had she already made up her mind and just assumed her friend would go along with it? She briefly considered telling Jasmin about the spell she attempted but realized there was no need. Especially if it didn't work. Jasmin would probably just scold her for being reckless.

When Sable had told them what was going on at Torie's housewarming party, Jasmin had been very empathetic, and Torie reminded her of that.

"Well, what was I going to say in the moment? I mean, I feel for the girl, but this is not something we need to get into."

"That's the same thing the witches in Trinity Cove told them. Am I missing something here? We have a friend who needs our help, and we are just going to turn our backs on them?"

Jasmin gave her a steely look and started to say something but then held her tongue.

"What? Go ahead, you can say whatever you want. Help me understand."

Jasmin bit the inside of her lip, and Torie could tell she was choosing her words carefully.

"Torie, I think that you are thinking with your heart and not your head. We don't know this werewolf. You are looking at this from the point of view of a woman who wants to help her boyfriend. And that by helping him, it ultimately helps you because it will make you feel better in your relationship with said boyfriend."

Torie didn't say anything but could feel a blush of crimson creeping up her neck and spreading to her cheeks.

"It's not that simple," she said. "The key player in this is Max's brother. He wants to kill Max, assume his role as alpha of their old pack. He will also kill Elric because he supported Max *and* because it will force Sable to then choose another fated mate. And guess who Max's brother wants that mate to be?"

Jasmin chewed on a scone as she regarded her friend.

"Jasmin, Max's own brother is going to kill him. We can't just stand by and watch."

Torie could practically read Jasmin's mind. She didn't need to say what was so obvious between them.

Jasmin sighed. "And of course, if anyone knows what it's like to have a sibling try to kill them, it's me."

"And just like I would never stand by and let that happen, I can't let it happen to Max either. And yes, if I'm being honest, I am thinking about myself as well. I love Elric and I don't want to lose him. In any way. I think if we don't do anything, then he's going to go on the run again. His loyalty to Max is beyond stubborn I think."

Jasmin huffed. "It isn't loyalty that would make him run, silly. If he were to take off it's to protect you. Werewolves are particularly vicious when it comes to vengeance on someone who has turned their backs on their own kind. If this wolf is willing to kill his own brother, what do you think he would do to someone else who crosses his path?"

Torie hadn't considered that. She only knew werewolves from her exposure to Elric and Max. Elric was so kind and gentle. Imagining him in some kind of bloodlust rage was not something she could picture.

"Tell you what," said Jasmin. "I'll consider this, but I want you to consider something for me as well."

Torie frowned. "Anything. You know that."

"Well, first wait to hear what it is. Come on, we're meeting Fionna at Jim's Bakery. She's a part of this as well."

Torie wasn't sure why her friend was being so vague, but she gathered her purse and followed her out the door.

Moonlight Hexes: Chapter Three

The inside of the bar known as Push Dagger, was dark and dank. The place smelled of mildew and vomit that had been washed away with only water. There was a juke box in the far corner that played a mix of eighties country and rock; at least when it worked that was what it played. The plastic bubble that shielded it from the open air was cracked in multiple places and dried blood was caked to the edge of it.

Like the men and women that frequented Push Dagger, the old juke box had seen better days.

A myriad of eyes looked up at the band of men that entered, taking them in with a quick, practiced sweep. Nostrils flared as the strangers' scents were pulled in by many of the bar patrons as well. Most went back to their drinks, or the intimate conversations they were engaged in. A few watched the band of men closely, giving them their full attention.

Arin Long Tooth stopped in the middle of the bar space, his men filing in around him. He tilted his head back and took a deep snort of the air, sorting the patrons by type and rank.

There were mostly shifters in the bar. He recognized what most of them were, but there were a couple who smelled of an animal he wasn't familiar with. There were a couple of banshees and a vampire that scurried out the back as soon as they walked in. Luckily, there were no humans to be found in the space.

Arin drew himself to his full impressive height. He was a massive man by all standards; over six and a half feet tall, pushing two hundred and sixty pounds of pure muscle. His eyes glinted in the dim light, and he let out a low feral growl.

A hush fell over the bar as everyone looked at him.

"I'm looking for a lost member of my pack," he said. "A woman by the name of Sable. Anyone here know her?"

Silence was the only answer he received as everyone went back to their business, ignoring the big werewolf. He growled again, feeling the shift about to come over him. These creatures needed to know who he was and understand that he wasn't someone to be ignored.

Before he could transform, a slight figure in a black hooded jacket stood up from the bar.

"I know who you're talking about," she said. "Calm yourself and have a seat. Let's talk."

Arin took in the tiny figure with more than just his eyes. She had no scent that he could discern, and that bothered him for some reason.

He turned to his beta. "Take the men and wait outside for me."

The beta looked at him questioningly, his eyes flitting from Arin to the smaller figure at the bar and back.

"The men are comfortable in here," he replied. "They might like a beer after the trek we just had."

Arin's eyes flashed a dangerous yellow and a rumble built in his chest.

"The men will be comfortable where I say they will be. And right now, I need them and you outside. Now go and wait for me until I come out."

The beta hesitated a brief moment before nodding and turning to the men. He motioned for them to follow him, and they filed out of the bar into the night.

Arin approached the bar and sat down next to the woman who had spoken up.

"I'm waiting," he said.

The woman barked a laugh. "Rather rude of your beta, don't you think? Has he always questioned you like that?"

Arin was taken aback but refused to acknowledge the question. The truth was, he was shocked at his beta's gall. Something was changing with him; it was subtle, but Arin could sense it.

"Oh well, not my problem," said the woman, taking a draw from her beer. "But you mentioned someone named Sable. I saw her. She's been here in Trinity Cove for a while. Or she was. Hot footed it out of here a few days ago with another…man."

Something about the way she said 'man' triggered a twitch in Arin. "What man? Where was she going?"

The woman shrugged. "I don't know who he was. But they were in a hurry. I can guess where she was going though, based on what she was looking for here."

Arin didn't speak. He was getting tired of this tiny person and had to rein in his wolf from biting her head off.

"She was asking around for witches here in town. Something about wanting them to break a bond she had or something like that. No witch would do it however, so my bet is she caught wind of a different breed of witch that lives up in Singing Falls. I'm betting she headed there to get them to do the deed."

Arin stiffened. His mind was spinning as he had an idea of who the other man was. He couldn't imagine why she might want her bond broken, and truthfully, he didn't care.

He knew who she was with, and it made his blood boil.

"Where is this Singing Falls?" he asked. "And what kind of supernaturals live there? Is it a town of darkness like this one?"

"Oh no. There are no towns like this one," she replied. "I can answer all your questions if you'll do something for me."

"What's that?"

"Take me with you."

He regarded the woman, not quite sure what to make of her request. "We need to travel fast. And we aren't babysitting anyone once we get there."

"Oh, trust me, I can keep up with you. And you needn't worry about taking care of me. If anything, I can help watch your back. From the witches up there. And maybe even your own little beta. Something new is in the air it seems. Shifters are acting…weird."

Arin looked at her, still unwilling to acknowledge what she was hinting at.

"You can come with me. But my business there is not pretty. Don't try to stop me or get in my way."

She turned to face him, her face twisting into a dark grin.

"Why, I wouldn't think of it. Besides, I have my own ugly business there as well."

Moonlight Hexes: Chapter Four

The bakery was all but deserted as the two of them entered. They found Fionna sitting in their usual spot; the large leather chairs that sat in front of the stone fireplace.

The squirrel shifter stood up and greeted her two friends with a hug.

"I ordered a round of elderberry muffins and two French presses for us," she said as the two witches settled into the chairs beside her.

Her eyes were sparkling and had that gleam that could only mean she was extremely excited about something.

"So, what's going on?" Torie asked.

"Well," said Jasmin, "look around you. Don't you just love this place?"

Torie looked around, taking in the space. There was nothing different about it; tables for two were arranged along one of the back walls. Small leather loveseats and chairs flanking gaming tables were dotted throughout the room as well. Everything was laid out in a way that invited a single person to sit and read or work on a laptop; or groups could gather to discuss the latest book they were reading or spread out and work on the latest project they might be knitting. It was a comfortable space that felt open and inviting, but never crowded. All the while, the smell of fresh baked bread, pastries of all kinds, and some of the best coffee in town, enveloped you like a cherished old blanket.

"Yes, I do love this place," Torie replied. "It was one of the first places you brought me to when I moved to town, and I fell head over heels for it. Though I will say it took me a lot longer to shed those extra pounds I put on from all these pastries than it would have taken me twenty years ago."

"Oh nonsense," said Fionna. "You look amazing. And I'm glad to see you're embracing that silver streak. It's very becoming on you."

At the mention of the stripe through her hair, Torie ran her fingers through it subconsciously, still not sure how she felt about it. Their encounter with Jasmin's treacherous sister had resulted in this, and nothing had worked to remove it. The fact that Fionna was complimenting her on it felt nice, but it also felt like she was being buttered up more than the breakfast biscuits the bakery was also known for.

"Thank you, Fionna. That means a lot. And can I just say that I would kill for your figure."

Fionna was blessed with a shifter's high metabolism that let her pretty much eat anything she wanted, whenever she wanted, and she never gained an ounce. Her figure was as lithe as a dancer's, and the shifter never seemed to run out of energy.

"Well, I think we can all agree that it's a beautiful bakery," said Jasmin, looking around.

Torie creased her brow. "Where is everyone? By now there should be a line out the door."

"So that's what I wanted to talk to you about," said Jasmin, just as their coffee arrived.

Typically, they would have heard their name called and then gone to the counter to pick up their order, but this time, Torie looked up to see Jim bringing it directly to them.

She was more than a little startled to see the owner serving them, but she thanked him profusely as he sat it down on the small coffee table next to their elderberry muffins.

"Well, have you…said anything?" he asked with a smile.

"Not yet," said Jasmin. "Give us a few, please."

Jim nodded and walked away, disappearing through an open door behind the counter.

"Jasmin, what's going on?" Torie asked again.

"The place is empty because it's closed today," said Jasmin. "Jim was kind enough to let us meet here to talk about something." She poured herself a cup of coffee and then one for Torie and Fionna before continuing. "He's selling this bakery, Torie, and moving down to Florida."

"What? Why?" asked Torie, putting down the cup she had just picked up.

"He's tired," said Fionna. "He's been here for thirty years and is ready to retire. It took a lot out of him when that golem caused a fight here amongst shifters. He just doesn't have the strength to keep going. So, he's selling and moving on."

"Okay, wow. I can understand that I guess. But what happens to this place?" Torie asked.

Fionna and Jasmin exchanged excited looks.

"Well, we were thinking that maybe we could buy it from him. Take it over," said Jasmin.

Torie was shocked as she regarded her friends.

Fionna piped up, her words practically tripping over themselves in excitement. "It would be a great opportunity for us. Well, for you I mean. I don't have any money so I can't help. At least not the kind of money you witches have; but I promise I would work day and night here and do anything you needed to make this place a success."

"Think about it, Torie. This bakery is a landmark here in Singing Falls. It's already established. We could make a few upgrades, maybe expand the lunch menu a little. And we could apply for a wine license."

"How long have you two known about this?" asked Torie.

"We just found out right before your housewarming party. And after tasting that amazing cake you made for Fionna's birthday, I knew this would be right up your alley. That cake needs to be available to the world, Torie. It was that good."

"Glen is still raving about it," added Fionna. "Just think, you could add your touch to the creations this place is known for."

Torie held up her hand.

"You don't have to sell me on this; you had me at wine."

Grab your copy...
vinci-books.com/moonlight

About the Author

M.J. Caan is an avid reader and writer of all things science fiction and fantasy. Author of multiple science fiction and paranormal fantasy series, M.J. likes to think that there is still magic out there in the world. Even if it's only between the pages of a great book.